CAUGHT IN A WEB

SANDEEP SHARMA

Srishti
PUBLISHERS & DISTRIBUTORS

Srishti Publishers & Distributors
A unit of AJR Publishing LLP
212A, Peacock Lane
Shahpur Jat, New Delhi – 110 049

editorial@srishtipublishers.com

First Published by
Srishti Publishers & Distributors in 2024

10 9 8 7 6 5 4 3 2 1

Printed and bound in India

Chapter 1
(Ahana)

Gone are the days when I was gripped with fear and despair at my predicament; I have now accepted this as my fate and continue to live my life that has become a long and tedious nightmare. Yes, a living nightmare. Calling it anything less than hell would be an injustice. I am forced to remain in a small and cramped room with a bed just big enough for one person and a chair shoved into the far corner of the room. There are no windows or clocks, and the walls are bare with no decorations or personal items. It's dark and dismal, and there's an oppressive feeling of being watched constantly. Someone is watching me. I can feel them constantly scrutinizing my every move. How can I forget about the CCTV camera? I'm sure someone is stalking me, but I don't know who or what they want from me.

I woke up painfully, my back screaming in agony as the lights flashed on. I looked up at the corner of the room to see the camera watching my every move. Rage coursed through me. I was filled with hatred for my captor. With a resigned sigh, I shuffled into the bathroom. It had become a disgusting habit to encounter the same bucket each day. I had to use it to bathe and relieve myself. It was often neglected and still bore the remains of the previous day's refuse clinging to its inside. The quantity of water was limited, so I had to use it wisely. I had no alternative. I was nothing more than a toy waiting to be sold off when the time was right.

Time had lost all meaning in this place. I did not know how many months or even years had elapsed since my abduction—it felt like an eternity now. My will to live had begun to ebb away, and I found myself unable to muster the energy to fight my captor anymore. I was nothing more than a puppet controlled by a master puppeteer, following their commands without complaint.

I am surrounded by a fog of confusion, unable to remember my past or who I really am. There are just flashes of events and scenes, but it all seems to be fading away slowly. The days of liberty feel as if they belonged to someone else, not me. Those memories are just stories that she whispers in my ears when I am asleep. I don't really like her. Initially, I thought she was one of the abductors, but when she told me about my past life, I learned that she was trying to help keep my memories alive. I tried a lot to meet, talk to, or at least see her, but she was afraid of the lights. She doesn't want to get caught by the person who is watching me; that's why she always comes to me when the lights are out.

Her name is Jasmeen, and she is my only friend in this room.

Chapter 2
(Randhir)

"Is she the one?" the man asked me after unzipping the body bag. The oppressive silence was like a thick fog smothering all sound until I heard nothing but the wild thumping of my own heart, beating faster with every passing second. I moved a few steps ahead to take a closer look, feeling all eyes pinned on me. The beaming luminosity of the room seared my eyes, blinding me with its intensity. I tried desperately to shut them, but I knew that if I did, this would be the last time I would ever see her. So instead, I blinked away the tears and stared into her face.

"Yes, she is my wife!" I didn't cry at all.

Cut to the present and I find myself in the same predicament again. "Is she the one?" I could still hear that man's voice, but this time, the man was not the same. He never was. Today, after 423 days and checking about 28 bodies, I had still not been able to identify her or find her. My heart pounded like a drum in my chest as I took a few steps closer. My body tensed, and then with a jolt, I stumbled backwards, tears streaming from my eyes. Fear threatened to overwhelm me as I struggled to regain control.

I said nothing. The man next to the body bag closed it again, and the inspector who accompanied me took me outside the morgue and tried to console me.

"Will I ever be able to find her? I don't know whether she is alive or..." I cried. The girl inside the body bag was not my daughter, but I was crying for the father of this girl, who still had no clue that his daughter had died. I can only hope that he did not need to wait for an eternity like me... 423 days and still counting.

"We are doing our best to find her, please keep faith. We'll find her." This is the third inspector on the case. The first one got promoted, and the other got suspended because of my complaint. I felt bad for the second one. I don't even remember his name now.

As I saw Parveen waiting for me in the waiting room, I felt a surge of guilt course through my veins. She had stuck with me after everything that happened, and here she was, still by my side. Part of me wanted to tell her to go, to convince her that it would be better for both of us if she ran away from this mess, but the other part of me selfishly wanted her around. I never found the strength to look into her eyes and make the tough decision to let her go.

"What happened?" she asked me with burning anticipation, but I was unable to answer. I continued my hasty steps to the exit. She stayed close behind me, desperately looking for an answer. We raced through the streets in an auto towards our house, a storm of questions hanging in the air.

Chapter 3
(Parveen)

When Randhir came back into my life, I thought that things would get better. I was in my mid-thirties and wanted to start my life anew, and I believed I was fortunate enough to get the love of my life back. How often does life present you with a second chance? I was indeed fortunate. After the death of my husband, I was all alone. It felt like I would never experience happiness again, but then Randhir reappeared in my life.

Randhir and I had been friends since college, but we never mustered up the courage to hold hands due to our traditional backgrounds. We both ended up getting married to different people.

Randhir and I had never gone through a wedding ceremony, but we simply began living together happily, or at least, that's what I thought. Perhaps Ahana didn't feel the same way. Ahana was Randhir and Nandini's daughter.

"Dad! How can you just bring a woman out of nowhere into our home and expect me to treat her as my mother?" I heard Ahana shouting on my first day at the house.

"I feel lonely. After your mother..." Randhir was trying to make his point when Ahana shut him up once again.

"Lonely? Just one year, Dad. She was alive and living in this

house just one year ago. How can you just move on in just one year? I wonder if you ever loved her, or were you just waiting for her to...." Ahana wanted to say the ugly thing, but before she could, Randhir slapped her hard, and she ran away. I still remember the words she uttered in a whisper while passing by me.

"I hate you. You can never be my mother."

Those were not just words; they were the foundation stones of my relationship with her.

Time marched on, but our relationship stayed frozen in place. I yearned for Ahana to look at me with love, but she kept herself aloof and just out of reach, and then...

"What is this commotion?" Randhir asked no one in particular when we were returning home from the hospital morgue. "Who the hell gave them information?" Rage surged through Randhir's veins as he watched the crowd of reporters swarm toward our auto. They were shouting out questions, jostling for the best spot to get the scoop, cameras and microphones at the ready. We could see in their eyes that they were all hungry for the sensational details of Meerut's mysterious case – the unsolved mystery of Ahana.

"Take the back lane, bhaiya," I yelled at the auto driver, and he floored the accelerator, desperate to avoid the crowd and comply with my command. Randhir was seething in anger, his voice rising to an ear-splitting pitch as he cursed the very existence of the media. I did all I could to try to calm him down, but it was useless against his overwhelming rage.

The media followed this case religiously, eager to spill every detail of the family's dark history into the public realm. The people of the city lapped up every intimate piece of information, treating our lives like prime-time entertainment. There was a time when even Randhir became the prime suspect and spent many nights in prison subjected to an interrogation that he never spoke about afterwards. There are some phases of life that are better forgotten.

As we crossed Mahesh's house, my apprehension was confirmed. He was standing outside his gate and smiling triumphantly.

"See, look at this bastard. I told you he will never change. He...he..." Randhir wanted to express his feelings, but rage rendered him speechless.

When we arrived home, Randhir rushed inside while I trailed closely behind. After paying the auto driver, I could hardly keep up with him as he hurried to the gate and dialled Mahesh's number on the phone.

"You fucking bastard! Why don't you just leave us alone?" Randhir barked into the phone. "It's all because of you that we're facing all this. You're the reason I still can't find my daughter or get some kind of closure. I beg you..." Randhir fell silent for a moment as he listened to Mahesh's response. Whatever Mahesh said caused Randhir to hang up the phone and take a seat in the nearby chair. Tears streamed down his face.

Chapter 4
(Mahesh)

"I am not the reason for anything. You started it. You were behind everything. Don't you dare blame it all on me! You and I both know the real truth. Don't force me to tell it to everyone." I slammed the receiver back into its cradle and leapt from my seat. I strode towards the window and pushed the curtains away, exposing the chaotic crowd of reporters outside. Seething with rage, I dropped into the rocking chair, feeling every movement like a tremor during an earthquake. My anger was not directed at the reporters, but at my fate—a fate that took the person I loved away from me. I tried calming myself down by taking deep breaths, but the memories of our happy times kept flooding my mind, making me feel more helpless and alone than ever before. As I sat there, lost in my thoughts, I couldn't help but wonder if life would ever be kind to me again.

I knew the reporter's expectations, but the words they wanted to hear wouldn't come out of my mouth today. I had already fed the media more than enough information, and now, in hindsight, I regret ever speaking up. I feel like a traitor for betraying the friendship that Ahana and I had shared, yet I was too desperate for the company since she vanished.

"I am sorry, uncle. I was just..." Ahana started to blabber when I caught her sneaking into my house. She was 13 years old back then.

"What are you doing here? Should I complain about you to your father? Where is he?" I was just looking for an excuse to fight him, and I thought I had found one.

I held Ahana's hand and dragged her outside when she said, "I came to see you, uncle. I have heard that you can talk to spirits."

"And who told you that?" I asked her and stopped suddenly.

"I saw that girl with whom you were talking a few days ago. She seemed to be possessed by a ghost, and my father also told me to stay away because you treat mad people, and you yourself are a bit..." Ahana stopped mid-sentence.

"Crazy...right?" I smiled at her uprightness. I invited her inside and made her sit on the sofa before my rocking chair. "So, do you believe in ghosts?"

"I had no idea about them, but then I saw her, and my mother told me a few stories, and now I am confused, but frankly... I still don't have any idea."

Ahana was a mature girl and conversed in a manner that was way beyond her age. She wore a white kurta along with a pair of blue jeans and white sneakers. She had her long, dark hair tied up in a ponytail. Her face was pale as moonlight, yet it radiated with confidence and intelligence. Her brown eyes twinkled when she talked, which made it difficult to concentrate on her words. She looked so innocent. I found myself lost in her beauty. I couldn't help but admire her charming smile. She was the epitome of elegance and grace, and I felt lucky to be in her presence.

"Does your mother believe in ghosts?"

"Yes, she does. She said that she had even seen a few in the village. They used to possess humans and talk about things which

were unknown to everyone, and...and...many other things." She ran out of words.

"So, you think that I am the person who gets the ghosts to leave these people's bodies, right?" I smiled.

"You look like one." She replied, and I couldn't control my laughter. She began to smile, too, and I could feel my heart warming up to her presence.

I saw her growing more confident and surer of herself with every passing minute. It seemed like she was born to talk; even though I had just met her that day, it felt like I had known her forever. We continued to talk for a long time. She had a way of making me feel comfortable, and I found myself opening up to her more than I usually would with someone new. Our conversation flowed effortlessly, and before we knew it, hours had passed by.

Since then, Ahana came to see me whenever her father wasn't home. She used to enjoy my lessons and was interested in psychology when I told her about my work. I assumed she was a curious child who was eager to learn new things, but I had no idea that she had something more in mind. She was holding back information from me. She needed assistance, but I was unaware of it until one day when she did the unexpected. It was her 17th birthday.

"What's the matter, Ahana? You seem to be a bit troubled. Is there anything I can help you with?" She started crying as soon as I spoke. I held her in my arms. She was just a child to me. I loved her like my granddaughter.

"I don't know why they don't just sort it out. Is it necessary to fight so loudly? I know they don't love each other, but why must it be shown to everyone? Why can't they pretend to be good parents? They should understand that they have a responsibility to handle." She stopped and cried again. I gave her a tissue.

Suddenly, she stood up from the sofa and went to see her reflection in the mirror on the opposite wall. She stared at the image as if she was seeing herself for the first time. She adjusted her hair a bit, then took a long breath, and continued, "Ahana couldn't sleep for the whole night. She was feeling afraid. She is not a strong girl. Her heart pounds so heavily when someone shouts in front of her. I somehow managed to console her."

I was dumbstruck! She was not Ahana. She was someone else.

I was jolted out of my thoughts when my phone started to ring. I stopped rocking my chair and noticed that the commotion outside my house had dispersed. I left the chair and grabbed the mobile. As I stood up, I felt a sharp stab of pain in my knees. I was an old man of fifty-five; the pain was merely a testament to the reality.

I shook my head and received the call, "I know your number, so please don't introduce yourself each time." He was the chief editor of TOI, Meerut, and I knew his number by heart now.

He laughed and replied, "So you must also be aware of the reason why I am calling?" He had the most idiotic and irritating voice.

"You are definitely very stubborn, Tanmay. It's been almost two years, and you still call me twice every month to ask me whether I have changed my mind. This must be appreciated, but trust me, now you only annoy me with these calls. I have told you that I have already shared a lot, and I don't want to share anything more about Ahana and her therapy."

"But, sir, what will you lose by sharing the case history with us? Who knows, it may help the police in some way," he reasoned.

"If the police need it, they can ask me for it. Now I request that you please don't call me again. Thank you." I hung up and really hoped he wouldn't bother me again.

I walked to the drawer next to the table and pulled out Ahana's photograph. She was seventeen years and seven months old when I clicked that photo. I couldn't resist kissing it. A drop of tear fell down my cheek.

"I miss you, Jasmeen," I said and continued looking at the photo.

Chapter 5
(Ahana)

"I know exactly what you want to do with her." I thought I heard her whisper in my ear. She was a ghostly presence standing next to me. I was jolted awake with a start, but when I searched around, she was nowhere to be found.

"What?" Ravi asked me in surprise. "Are you alright?" He put his hand on my knee. He was trying to be casual, as I was wearing a white floral dress that ended just above my knee. I immediately felt uncomfortable and quickly moved his hand away. It was a clear violation of my personal space and boundaries.

"Yeah, I am fine. Just a bit tipsy." The music was very loud, and the lights were quite dim. My mind was swirling with the beats. It was my first time at the disco. We were having the unofficial 'Promoted to Second Year' party. Everywhere I looked, people were dancing and swaying to the rhythm of the music. The air was thick with excitement and anticipation as everyone waited for the next song to be played. I watched as couples swayed on the dance floor and embraced each other lovingly while singing along to their favourite tunes. People's eyes lit up when they saw each other, and hugs were exchanged. But contrary to the vibes, where everything looked joyful and energetic, I was in no mood to stay longer. Kiran's constant nagging had made me come to the party. She was my best friend; the one who had looked at me all emotionally and said, "We won't be getting these days back. From tomorrow, we all become part of the race called life." That's how she had convinced me to come along, and now she was nowhere to be seen. I sat at the corner table with Ravi, who had been glued to me since my arrival. His gaze was predatory, his eyes never straying from the curve of my breasts since I had arrived at the party. I could see the saliva pooled in the corner of his mouth as he hungrily devoured me with his eyes. I couldn't shake the feeling that I was nothing more than a piece of meat to him.

"I think I should go now. I am feeling sleepy." I told Ravi and tried to stand up, but he pulled me down. I wanted to slap him, but suddenly I felt powerless. My heart was racing, and my mind was in a state of confusion.

"The party has just begun. You can't leave this early." He stood up from his seat and sat next to me. His hands were reaching for my top. A shiver ran down my spine as his touch sent electricity through my body. I knew I had to stop him, but I was frozen in place, unsure of what to do next. I tried to resist him, but suddenly sleep took over me.

I heard Jasmeen. Yes, somehow, she had managed to come to the party as well. She took Ravi with her, and they danced like crazy. They moved together like they were possessed, their bodies entwined in a primal frenzy that left me feeling both exhilarated and envious. As I watched them, I could feel my own pulse quicken with desire, and for a moment, it felt like we were all part of some twisted fever dream that refused to let us go. I thought I was dreaming all of it, but it all appeared so vivid and real, and it was not the first time.

"I know exactly what you wanted to do with her," Jasmeen told Ravi, leaning in and whispering into his ears as the music was too loud. Ravi was wearing some kind of cheap perfume, which mixed with the sweat and was a nightmare for Jasmeen's nostrils. I could smell it as well.

Ravi seemed confused about everything.

"Let's go up and fulfil your desires." Jasmeen took Ravi with her. They tumbled onto the sofa in a heated embrace, their lips locked together as if it was their last kiss. The fire of their passion ignited as they tore away each other's clothing, revealing what had once been forbidden. Jasmeen felt no fear or shame as Ravi looked into her eyes, his expression uncertain. Then suddenly, the music died, leaving them suspended in a moment of pure, desperate intensity. Then, suddenly, Ravi realized the presence of someone totally unwelcome.

"Shit...shit...shit! Run Ahana." Ravi gathered all his clothes and started running. Suddenly my eyes opened, and I found myself sitting on the sofa, my clothes disoriented.

"Sir, she is high." Some women came and stood near me. She appeared to be a police officer. She was saying something, but I couldn't hear her properly. I don't know when I fell into a deep sleep once again.

* * *

I was dreaming that I was travelling to a police station with other boys and girls my age, but when I opened my eyes, I found myself sitting in a corner behind bars. I felt a chill run down my spine as I realized that it was not a dream, but a nightmare come true. I wondered how I had ended up behind bars. I was actually in a police station. I looked around myself, bewildered because I had no recollection of why or how I had reached here. I was feeling thirsty. I wanted to speak, but I felt my throat was dry. I found a water pot in another corner of the cell and rushed to grab some water for myself. The pot was empty. I looked around to see if there was any water source nearby, but I couldn't find any.

I grabbed the iron bars, looked into the eyes of one of the constables, and pleaded, "I need a glass of water, please."

"The dinner is almost ready, madam. We'll serve the water with it. Should I clean the table for you as well?" The lady in khaki replied and then snapped, "Shut the fuck up and sit down."

I got scared and sat back on the stone slab. There were six other girls with me in the cell, and they all started laughing at me. I felt embarrassed and ashamed, but I knew showing fear would only worsen things. I decided to close my eyes and drift back to sleep because that is what I have always done in my life. I run from situations where I feel scared. I closed my eyes and sensed that I was trembling at one second and not at another. Jasmeen came to my rescue.

"What are you doing to her?" I heard Jasmeen's voice when a girl tried to touch me inappropriately when the lights went off at night. I knew it was happening to me. I was just afraid. I didn't push that girl back. I knew if I opened my eyes, Jasmeen would never come out to rescue me. I could only hear her. I never saw her.

Jasmeen abruptly awoke and slapped the girl sleeping next to her. The sudden sound reverberated through the cell, waking all the other inmates. They erupted in a cacophony of protests until a female police officer on night duty arrived and banged her stick against the iron bars.

"Oye, you two. Come out." She called Jasmeen and the other girl out. The lady constable opened the door for us and took us out to the next cell.

"Madam, don't slap this new girl in the face. She looks quite like a heroine." One of the girls in the cell commented when

Jasmeen came out of the cell. All the other girls laughed.

"Don't worry, Ahana. I am with you. Keep your eyes closed." Jasmeen whispered to me. I nodded vigorously.

"What did you say?" The lady constable asked Jasmeen.

"Nothing. I was talking to Ahana." Jasmeen replied.

"Your name is Ahana?" The lady constable asked the other girl, whom Jasmeen had just slapped.

"No, madam. My name is Suruchi," the girl replied.

"Then who is Ahana?" She asked Jasmeen again.

"I am Ahana. It was Jasmeen who hit this girl. Please leave me. I am innocent." I opened my eyes, and I saw that Jasmeen had vanished. I was trembling in fear, and watching the wooden stick in the lady's hand made me sweat heavily.

"She is doing drama, madam. I think she is indeed some heroine of some cheap production house," Suruchi commented.

"Let me speak, Ahana. You keep your eyes closed." Jasmeen whispered to me, and I closed my eyes again. The trembling was gone.

"What is happening to you? Who are you?" It was the lady constable's turn to feel strange. She was feeling nervous now.

"I am Jasmeen. Didn't she just tell you about me? I slapped this fucking girl. She was trying to touch Ahana, and I won't let her do that. I would slap her all night if she tried to do that again." Jasmeen charged towards the girl, and out of reflex, the lady constable swung her baton, which landed on Jasmeen's thighs. It hurt.

"I am sorry, madam. Please let us go." I opened my eyes because the pain was excruciating. I couldn't keep my eyes closed with such pain.

"What the... are you mad or what?" The lady constable was confused. I had seen that look many times. It was difficult for people with low IQs to differentiate between Jasmeen and me. I was told by my ghost-buster uncle.

"Madam, I think she is a runaway from some mental hospital," Suruchi commented.

"Mental hospital? No, ma'am, please don't send me back. I beg of you. That is not a hospital... I will apologize on behalf of Jasmeen. I will not close my eyes, I promise. Jasmeen won't come. I'll keep her controlled, but don't send me back to Divya Hospital. That place is hell... I beg you, madam, please don't send me to Divya Hospital."

Chapter 6
(Randhir)

"I want to express my sorrow at the difficult position you find yourself in. Please believe me when I say that it pains me deeply, but as a businessman, I have no other choice." Mr Digvijay Singh Rathore, the business tycoon of Meerut, shifted uneasily on the worn and creaking sofa. He looked around the room with disdain at the few pieces of tattered, stained, and aged furniture. He could see the broken windows, the damp walls, and the dirt-soaked floor. He had asked me many times to visit his office for a face-to-face meeting, but I had refused each time. I wanted nothing more to do with the man who had made Ahana's life a living nightmare. However, Digvijay knew how to use people and manipulate situations to his own advantage. Despite my desire to cut ties with Digvijay, I couldn't help but feel a sense of unease, knowing that he could potentially cause harm. Parveen was the sole bread earner and Digvijay was her boss. "I'm glad you allowed me to come here and see you in person."

"You know exactly why I have given you permission to come and sit in my drawing room. I don't want to hear your bullshit and your empty words. We both know what kind of monster you are. Please don't pretend and come straight to the point," I snapped back. I wanted this to end as soon as possible.

"Permission?" Digvijay laughed sarcastically. I was seething with anger. I couldn't believe his audacity. I took a deep breath and tried to calm myself.

Parveen intervened, coming to my rescue, "Digvijay sir, I want you to please come to the point. You asked me to arrange this meeting. I had to convince Randhir a lot to agree to this. Please don't make things worse for us."

Yes, she was the reason why I had agreed to meet this person. My wife, Parveen, was taking care of Digvijay's disabled son as a full-time nurse. She had been forced to arrange this meeting in order to keep her job at his house. Parveen told me everything, and out of fear of losing the only source of money that we had to pay our bills, I had agreed to meet Digvijay. Despite feeling uneasy about the situation, a meeting with Digvijay was our only option if we wanted to keep her job and our financial stability.

"I am here to know where is Ahana. I am quite sure that you know where she is, but you are hiding it from everyone out of fear of losing your daughter." Digvijay's voice had a strange menacing quality. It continued to linger in the space long after he had spoken. People often found themselves drawn to his voice as if captivated by it. Every word he spoke carried weight and importance that demanded attention. But all these qualities left no impression on me. I just felt an inexplicable surge of anger the moment I saw him.

"Are you out of your mind?" I was putting all my strength and resources into trying to find my daughter and weeping and praying all day and night in the hope of finding her, and this man was accusing me of faking all of that. "Do you really think that I would sit here waiting if I had the slightest idea where my daughter was? Am I fooling people around? Do I look like that kind of person to you? And...and what is the motivation for doing all this? I was living my life... I was happy with everything

I had... I had my daughter right here with me... Why would I make her disappear for no reason at all?"

My body was wracked with uncontrollable tremors as an icy chill spread through my veins. I was overcome and consumed by emotions. Parveen's tight grip on my hand didn't seem to help, and I could feel tears stinging my eyes, threatening to burst forth any second.

"Motivation..." Digvijay smiled and looked at Parveen. Parveen had no expression on her face. "Motivation...huh... okay, let's talk about that. What about avoiding arrest? Does that sound good enough as motivation for making your daughter disappear?" He paused and my mouth fell open in disbelief at hearing his words. He continued, "Or worse... What about your daughter going back to the mental hospital from where you bailed her out? Do you think I don't know about the lives of the people who work for me? Do you think I am a fool? Do you think I don't know what happened to Parveen just one day before Ahana disappeared?"

The moment I met Parveen's gaze, my heart sank. She had spoken about that incident to someone else and all this time, she had kept it a secret from me. This deception tore away at the last vestiges of my trust in people. I could see that she was apologetic and regretful as she stood there silently, tears streaming down her cheeks. However, all I could feel at that moment was a surge of red-hot rage coursing through my veins. I struggled to control my emotions and not lash out at her, but the hurt and betrayal were too much to bear. I needed time to process my feelings. But before any of that, I needed to confront Digvijay and get him out of my house.

"Whatever happened in my house is my own business; why are you getting involved in it? What made you come and ask for

Ahana? What is there for you in it?" I asked Digvijay, leaning forward to stare into his eyes, to let him know that he may have gained access to the secrets of my house, but that didn't mean he could do anything he wanted.

Digvijay unbuttoned his coat, brought out a bunch of papers from the inner pocket, and kept it on the table. I looked at them and felt confused. "I am a businessman, and make no mistake, I will do whatever it takes to protect my business. Those papers you signed last time, you better read them again—especially clause three. The police have a copy, too, though you were never informed because I asked them to keep it hushed. So far, I've stayed silent on the 'motivation' we talked about earlier, but if you fail to tell me anything you find out about Ahana, I won't be able to guarantee my silence any longer."

Digvijay was now on his way out when he stopped abruptly and dialled some number. I could hear the bell ringing, and then finally, Digvijay spoke. "Mahesh, how are you? Do you know it is a bad habit to eavesdrop on neighbours? Also, there is no child in this house anymore. Don't waste your energy here. You can find children in the park, playing all around. Go there and enjoy."

Mahesh did not say anything. He simply cut the call.

"I'll be meeting you again soon." Digvijay waved his hand and left our house.

I came out following him. I saw Mahesh standing and staring at Digvijay with furious eyes. Mahesh's fists were clenched, and his body was tense as if he were ready to attack Digvijay. I could sense the tension between them and knew that something had happened. Digvijay laughed like a maniac when his phone rang. He accepted the call while opening the gate of his car. Suddenly he stopped smiling and said, "Keep me informed. I am on my way."

Chapter 7
(Parveen)

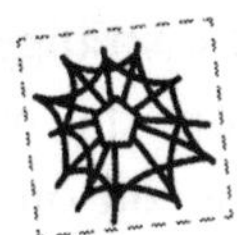

As Randhir slammed the door shut, I sensed that something horrible was about to happen. In a flash, he charged at me like a wild beast and pinned me against the wall with a vice-like grip around my neck. His breath was hot against my face as he snarled, “Didn’t I tell you to keep your mouth shut? Didn’t I tell you not to talk to Digvijay about anything that happened in my house? What part of my warning didn’t you understand?”

I was unable to speak, choked up and struggling to breathe. I tried to form words and deliver them, but nothing came out. I gasped for air, knowing that I would collapse in the next few seconds. Randhir realized my struggle and let me go. I took a deep breath, filling my lungs with much-needed oxygen. I was on my knees, trying to gather my thoughts. Digvijay’s arrival and his mention of the night we spent in this house, just a day before Ahana’s disappearance, had shaken Randhir. He had not expected that betrayal from me, but he did not know what I was going through. I had to relieve myself in one way or another.

“I’m sorry, Randhir, but I had no choice. I had to tell him. I was afraid for myself and Ahana,” I said, panting. I tried to stand and hug Randhir because I knew he needed someone to hold him. His steely demeanour may have fooled the world, but

I knew the truth. Inside, Randhir was nothing but a frightened child, his fragile ego on the verge of shattering at any moment. Our marriage had been a living hell, filled with Randhir's abusive outbursts. But only I knew the reason behind his violent temper—his unbridled love for Ahana. Apart from what people knew about Ahana and her 'issue', as we call it at home, she was also very stubborn and had a strange attitude. Randhir had no control over Ahana, and now the frustration of having raised a spoiled child was taking a toll on him. Randhir was getting weaker with every passing day. I had seen him lose his temper in front of Ahana many times, but he stayed silent because of the love he had for her.

"How is it?" Randhir asked Ahana with a bright smile on his face as she took the first bite of Paalak Paneer, her favourite dish that he had cooked for her on her twentieth birthday.

"Your dad cooked all of this for you. He has been in the kitchen since morning, and I wanted to tell Ahana what her father did for her," I said, but before I could finish, Ahana slammed the spoon down on the table.

"This is bad—worse than it could ever be. You can never match the skills of my mother in cooking, and you..." Ahana finished with her father, then pointed her finger at me, saying, "You are not allowed to speak directly to Ahana ever." She was enraged. It felt awkward when she referred to herself in the third person, but that's how she behaved sometimes. It was particularly uncomfortable for me since I was new to the house and had only known Ahana for a few weeks.

Ahana left the table and rushed outside. Randhir sat at the dining table, motionless and silent. I felt heartbroken for him, as he had put in hours to make Ahana's birthday special, but she had no respect for anything. I took the chair next to Randhir, took a bite of the food he had made, and said, "This is delicious. I love the food." I smiled at him.

He raised his head, looked straight into my eyes, and with no expression on his face, said, "Does it matter? Did I cook for you? It was all just a waste of time." He screamed and toppled the whole dining table.

I was in shock. Tears welled up in my eyes. Randhir stormed off to his room in anger. I stayed in the dining room for a while until I heard him sobbing. I gathered the courage to face him and, when I reached him and saw him crying on the bed, I couldn't help but hug him and console him.

Today, I wanted to do the same. I wanted to console him. But he was still angry. He let out an animalistic roar before violently snatching the flowerpot off the stool and slamming it down with a deafening crash that shook the very foundations of the house. I recoiled in horror at the sight of him, possessed by rage like never before.

"I am sorry, Randhir. Please forgive me. I was afraid. I hope you understand what it must have felt like to me. I could have died. You know how she treated me, and I wished her well. I just had to inform..." I wanted to buy some time for myself and wait until he calmed down.

Randhir sat on the sofa and picked up the papers that he had left on the table. I knew what they were. It was the agreement between Ahana and Divya Mental Hospital that Randhir had signed when he forcefully took Ahana out of there.

"I'm sorry, but I don't think I'm making myself clear here," Digvijay said as he sat in his office, with Randhir and me sitting across from him. A large table separated Digvijay from us, with only a laptop and a nameplate that read, 'Digvijay Singh Rathore, Managing Director, Divya Mental Hospital. "She is still being

treated and is a danger to society. She doesn't know what she will do or say when she 'transforms' into Jasmeen. She poses a danger to everyone around her," he explained.

"I understand what you're saying, but please, I beg of you, understand this. I'm happy to do anything in return. I want my daughter back. I can't live without her," Randhir pleaded, his hands folded. I did the same. "Please, sir. We'll do anything to have her back," I added. Digvijay looked into my eyes, silently conveying what he wanted. I lowered my gaze.

"Okay. If that's what you want, you have to sign a few papers for me, and my secretary outside will explain the details to you," Digvijay said as he got up from his chair. We followed him out, and he turned to face me. "And you, I want you to meet me at the house in the evening. I need to discuss a few things about my son's health." I nodded obediently. Randhir smiled as Digvijay left, and the secretary handed us a few agreement papers.

"What is this about?" Randhir asked as the secretary gave him the papers.

"There are a few points I want to highlight before you sign these papers. This agreement is related to Ahana and her behaviour. Firstly, you need to visit the hospital every week for regular checkups. You have to keep the medication running as per the doctor's prescription. Ahana is not allowed to leave the city without prior notice to the hospital, and the most important part is clause 3, which you can read thoroughly," the secretary explained.

Randhir read the point aloud: "If anything happens to Ahana, or she becomes violent towards someone or causes harm to anybody, the hospital will take no responsibility for it and can intervene at any point in time and take the patient back to observation and treatment." He nodded and signed the papers.

"Do you know what they did to Ahana? Have you heard about the things she revealed that happened to her? It was all the hospital's fault. They weren't treating her, they just wanted to keep her, so that... so that...," Randhir wasn't able to complete before tears started to stream down his face. "And we gave them a clean chit to take our daughter back. They put that clause in deliberately. I knew it. They just want my daughter back. I'm glad she's gone."

"But they wanted to treat her, Randhir. Why else would they want to take her back? They knew she was ill. She tried to kill me, Randhir. You know that! Ahana wanted me to die."

Chapter 8
(Ahana)

I recognized the room instantly. It was the same one I had spent countless days in before. I knew every detail: the table, the chair, the filthy bed, and the CCTV that watched me 24/7. But this time, I wasn't alone. Jasmeen was with me, and her presence comforted me.

I spent three to four hours in complete darkness until the lights flashed on suddenly, hurting my eyes. The only door in the room burst open, and there stood Digvijay with his creepy smile.

"You were good, my girl. I suspected you would last a maximum of six months, but you did great in hiding," he said, taking the only chair in the room and adjusting himself in it. "One and a half years! That's brilliant work."

"Sir, please let me go. Call my father. He is my guardian. You can't take me back to the hospital. You signed the papers yourself," I pleaded, trying to summon my courage.

"Ahana..." Digvijay sighed in disappointment. "I am not in the mood to talk to you. Go to sleep and call Jasmeen. Hurry up. I don't have time. Otherwise, I'll give you electric shocks. Come on...speed up the process."

His order was impossible to execute, but I tried to follow it, anyway. How could I sleep in these circumstances? My life had become a cruel joke, and I was trapped like an animal. But then, almost instantly, I fell asleep, and Jasmeen took over.

"I knew that Parveen was helping you out." It was Jasmeen's voice.

"It's wonderful to meet you, Jasmeen. I never doubted your intelligence. You're something special. And by the way, she is your mother. Don't call her by her name," Digvijay said, now elated. His face lit up as he spoke. His eyes sparkled, and he really seemed to be enjoying this conversation.

"She is Ahana's stepmother. She means nothing to me," Jasmeen retorted. Her face was emotionless, but her voice was full of disdain and anger.

"I love it! I love your anger. I was just checking if you're still passionate inside. People are going to love you even more."

Digvijay got up, walked over, and kissed Jasmeen on the head. It felt wet and disgusting to me.

"People will love this...start screaming and let the dark world know that Jasmeen is back," he said, addressing no one in particular. He was about to leave when I woke up and asked, "Will I ever see my father again? Could you please at least let him know that I am alive?" I pleaded.

"I'm sorry, love. But you're dead to the world," Digvijay replied, leaving the room and closing the door behind him.

It was six months after I had returned home from the hospital at my father's request when Parveen set me up. It was a normal day until dinner time. As usual, we sat in silence, with nothing to talk or discuss. After we finished eating, we went to our respective rooms. I tried to study, but my mind kept wandering. Then, I heard someone in the hallway outside my door. I left my chair and went out. It was completely dark outside. I headed towards the kitchen to get some water, and on the way, I passed

Parveen's room. Parveen and my father had separate rooms while I was there.

As I passed by Parveen's room, it felt strange. The room was slightly ajar and completely dark. It felt empty. A sudden urge to sneak a peek inside grew in me. I had never seen her room before, as it was always closed. As I moved towards the room, someone pushed me from behind, and I fell straight into the bed inside. The lights came on, and I saw that it was Parveen who had pushed me in. I was about to say something when she started to breathe heavily and shout.

"Randhir... Randhir...someone save me," Parveen shouted as I entered the hallway outside her room. Confused, I asked her why she had pushed me into her room and why she was acting so strange. My father came running to see what was going on, only to find Parveen crying as she ran and hugged him tightly. She accused me of trying to kill her by suffocating her with a cushion and begged my father to send me back to the hospital. Despite my protests that Parveen was lying, my father ordered me to go back to my room. Angry and frustrated, I complied.

That night, Jasmeen whispered to me, "I told you earlier, they hate you. You're just a burden to them. Trust me, and run away. I'll help you. I even have a plan." For the first time, I trusted Jasmeen's words and decided to run away from home. I realized that she was the only one who had stood by me when I needed someone. I couldn't bear the thought of going back to the hospital, and I knew that Parveen wanted me to go so that she could regain my father's attention. That bitch just wanted to steal my father away from me.

Chapter 9
(Mahesh)

"Mahesh, how are you? Do you know it is a bad habit to eavesdrop on neighbours? Also, there are no children in this house. Don't waste your energy here. You can find children in the park playing all around. Go there and enjoy," Digvijay's words rang in my ears.

I knew his car's number. I saw him at Randhir's house, and my hatred for him drew me there. I hated Digvijay more than Randhir and anything else in this world because he was the one who took everything from me – my career, my image, and my family. By the grace of God, I had Jasmeen with me, but this rascal took away that one joy left in my life as well.

How could a man be so cruel? How could a man stoop so low? How had I wronged him? I was just doing my duty, giving his son the treatment he needed. What was wrong with that? I am still searching for answers, but I can't seem to find any.

My eyes were fixed on Digvijay when I saw him coming out of Randhir's house and then moving forward to his car. His face brought all the memories back. That horrible day of my life when things went so wrong that I lost everything I valued in life.

"Ajay, is there something you need to discuss with me?" I asked the 9-year-old patient seated in front of me. His teachers had

requested a second opinion on his mental health, as he had shown early signs of dyslexia and was a slow learner. However, when I asked his parents for his medical history, they didn't respond. They were afraid that if people found out he was seeing a psychiatrist, it would ruin their business's image. Ajay was Digvijay's son.

"You'll get into trouble if I tell you anything. It's about my dad. He wants to kill..." Ajay started to say, but Digvijay barged into my house before he could finish his sentence.

"How dare you? Didn't I tell you to stay away from my son?" Digvijay yelled.

"He was sent here by his teachers. I didn't bring him here. Besides, I can obtain a court order if you refuse to let me treat your child. I don't want things to get ugly. Let me treat your son. We can keep everything confidential," I tried to reason with Digvijay.

"Confidential, huh? If I remember clearly, you have a granddaughter, right? Do you love her?" Digvijay asked menacingly.

"Yes, I do. Why are you asking?" I was perplexed.

"Do you want her to leave you all alone?" Digvijay threatened.

"What do you mean?"

"Because I know some things about you that are confidential. If they are leaked to the public..." Digvijay paused briefly and looked at me pitifully, "I'm sorry for your loss in advance, Mahesh."

The next day, I found myself on the front pages of all the newspapers and news channels. One of my patients had falsely accused me of being a paedophile. I knew that it was all Digvijay's doing, but the news spread rapidly, and I lost everything. I can still recall that heartbreaking phone call from my son.

"Dad?"

"Son, thank God you called. The news is all fake...it is all..." I began to plead over the phone to explain myself, but he interrupted me.

"Dad...listen... I'm calling to inform you that I'm leaving for New York with my family. It's becoming suffocating for me to explain it to everyone. I hope you'll understand."

"Family? Am I not your family, son?"

"Dad...bye."

I was silently rocking in my chair, thinking about the past, which was the only activity that gave me some solace these days when my phone rang. I looked at the caller ID, there was no name, but I knew the number. It was the reporter again.

"Tanmay, what is your problem?" I felt pity for him sometimes. He was so desperate for his work, but I had nothing more to share with him. I had my own reservations as well.

"Hello, sir. How are you?" He replied in his cheerful voice.

"I am fine and have nothing to share, as usual. So please, Tanmay, get a grip and search for something else. I am sure there are many stories in this town that are waiting to be explored." I was about to hang up when he spoke.

"Wait, sir, this time I have something to share with you, and let me tell you, this is exclusive information. I have almost risked my life to get it for you."

"What information?" He had my complete attention now. He took his time to reply.

"The police are thinking of closing the case."

"What rubbish? They can't do that."

"They are planning to do so. They have not received any concrete evidence that Ahana is alive, and that's why they are..."

"But Ahana is alive.... I mean, somewhere, she is...waiting for us. I can feel that." I tried to hide my real emotions.

"The police don't work like this, sir. They need evidence, and the evidence is almost indicating that Ahana is dead and..." I hung up the phone, got on my feet, and started to pace around the room. I was getting anxious. My mind suddenly started throwing numerous images and ideas at me, and I was unable to process any of them.

I went to the kitchen, took a glass of water, and silently drank it. Then I rushed to my laptop and opened the website of the State Bank of India. I logged in with the details and looked at the transaction of an account number. Suddenly, fear started to grow within me. How could this be possible? There have been no transactions from the bank account since last week.

Jasmeen was definitely in some danger.

Chapter 10
(Parveen)

I married Randhir when Ahana was twenty years old. I wanted us to be the perfect family, but Ahana never accepted me. I knew there was something that Randhir was trying to cover up... some truth about Ahana, as he was so protective of her. While I could understand Ahana's hatred, Randhir's strange behaviour was something that I didn't understand until the day I heard Jasmeen's voice.

"How can you be so stupid? She doesn't love you. She cares only about your father. He killed your mother for her. Don't you remember what happened on that terrace? Just don't use your brain," I heard Ahana's voice coming from her room as I passed by at night. I wondered whom she was speaking to as she had no friends to talk to on the phone. I leaned against the door, trying to open it, but it was locked from inside. I decided to eavesdrop.

"But Jasmeen, she looks so friendly. And you know how my mother was..." Ahana spoke again, her voice changing in texture.

"You don't know how people behave. They're all two-faced. You do not know how cruel the world is. Love can make you evil. Love is the poison of sanity. It drags you to hell." Ahana spoke again, and it was then that I realized that she was talking to herself. I was worried about her and knew what I had to do. I confronted Randhir that very same night.

"Randhir, we need to talk about Ahana," I said.

"What?" he was defensive, as always.

"You know she's ill, but you're still keeping her locked inside the walls of your home. Do you think that will help her? How long can you keep her locked up? One day, she will need to go out, and then what will happen to her?" I tried to reason with him.

"What are you talking about?" he continued to hide things.

"I just heard her. She's suffering from Multiple Personality Disorder, and I think you know about it, but you're trying to hide the fact that she needs medical attention." I sat next to him on the bed.

He was silent, not reacting to my words.

"She's being poisoned by her own unconscious thoughts. She named the other personality inside her Jasmeen, and now Jasmeen is trying to feed Ahana's mind with lies about the accident that happened with your first wife," I said, finally grabbing his attention as I mentioned the incident.

"What did you hear?" he asked, looking straight into my eyes.

"She thinks it was you who pushed your wife from the terrace that day. Jasmeen is making her believe that you did this to marry me. You killed your first wife so that you could marry me," I said.

It felt strange to utter those words because it was not only Jasmeen who had this opinion, but almost everyone suspected Randhir to be the killer of his first wife; even the police. It was hard for Randhir to bear everything. He had loved his first wife just as he loved me now, but the world failed to see the love in his eyes. Randhir started to sob, crying like a baby. I took him in my arms, trying to give him strength.

"You can't help Ahana by keeping her locked up. She needs medical attention. Trust me, I'll talk to Digvijay sir and get the best possible treatment for her at Divya Hospital. She'll always be under my guidance, and I'll keep an eye on her. She'll get better soon," I assured him.

The very next day, I talked to Digvijay sir, and he agreed to admit Ahana to the hospital. It took around three weeks for Ahana to get accustomed to the procedure and for the doctors to understand her medical condition fully. Once the roadmap to her recovery was laid down, the doctors moved her to a more private chamber. I didn't let Randhir know that Ahana was no longer under my watch, as I knew he would panic.

Ahana was now in a private chamber where only doctors were allowed. Randhir and I visited her twice a week, but we usually found her asleep due to the heavy medication she was on. She found it difficult to understand our words, and she appeared quite helpless.

"Ahana, how are you feeling? Is there anything you want to say to us? Are they treating you well? Beta, talk to me," Randhir pleaded while we were visiting her. Ahana looked like a zombie, pale and sleepy. She looked at us as if trying to figure out who we were.

"Dad?" she said after a long pause.

"Yes, beta. Tell me. I am your dad. What is it? Tell me," Randhir said.

"How can you just let me go through all this?" Ahana strained to speak.

"They don't let me sleep at night. I want to sleep. I don't know where they will take me tonight. Last night, they tried to rape me, but then I slept as I couldn't bear it. I don't know what they did to me then. Dad, can I sleep now?" Ahana murmured. Randhir lost his cool. He stormed straight into Digvijay sir's office. After all, it was a matter of his daughter's safety!

"What are you doing to my daughter? What is happening to her? Who the fuck tried to touch my daughter?" Randhir shouted.

Digvijay was caught unaware and didn't recognize Randhir at first, but then he saw me and got hold of the situation.

He called the doctor inside, and the doctor said, "We are keeping her on a heavy dosage, and during this, she sleeps a lot. While sleeping, she dreams a lot. So often, she confuses her dreams with reality. This happens with patients a –"

The doctor's explanation was cut short as Randhir slammed the table in front of Digvijay and said, "I want my daughter back. Enough of your hospital and medication."

This was the beginning of the animosity between Digvijay and Randhir. Randhir pulled every string to get Ahana back from the hospital. He was like a possessed man with only one ambition in life – to get his daughter back home. Digvijay took this as an assault on his ego and decided to take revenge. He started monitoring Ahana and keeping an eye on her.

Chapter 11
(Mahesh)

Everyone has a secret, and I, too, had one. For nine years, I tried to hide it from everyone because it was the only thing left for me to cherish in life. Digvijay ruined my life by accusing me of being a paedophile. I was all alone; my son, daughter-in-law, and granddaughter – they were the only family I had, and they left me because of the smear campaign Digvijay led. He took everything from me.

Only a decade ago, I was the most successful person in my field and my life was perfect. I had a wonderful family, I was earning a fortune and was the most respected psychiatrist in the country. I was the star of my profession, but in just one day, everything changed. A single newspaper headline, a false allegation without any proof, turned all my achievements to dust. I was broken.

The silence was deafening. I was rocking on my chair, all the lights were off, and I could hear the wind blowing. There was nothing in my mind, and I was clueless about what to do. I think I hadn't had any food that day when I heard a strange voice from the window that faced the garden area. Someone had jumped into the garden, which alarmed me.

I am sorry, uncle. I was just…" Ahana started to blabber as soon as I caught her sneaking into my house. She was thirteen years old back then.

"What are you doing here? Should I complain to your father about you? Where is he?"

"I came to see you, uncle. I heard that you can talk to spirits."

"And who told you that?" I asked her and stopped suddenly. There was a strange innocence in her eyes. She reminded me of my granddaughter. She was just five years old when she was taken away from me to America, and I missed her the most.

"I saw that girl with whom you were talking a few days ago. She seemed to be possessed by a ghost, and my father also told me to stay away because you treat mad people, and you yourself are a bit..." Ahana stopped in between.

"Crazy, right?" I smiled at her straightforwardness. I invited her inside and made her sit on the sofa in front of my rocking chair. "So you believe in ghosts?"

"I had no idea about them, but then I saw her, and my mother told me a few stories. Now, I am confused, but frankly... I still don't have any idea." Ahana was a mature girl and conversed in a manner that was way beyond her age.

"Does your mother believe in ghosts?"

"Yes, she does. She said that she even saw a few in the village. They used to possess human souls and talk about things that were unknown to everyone, and many other such things." She ran out of words.

"So, you think that I am the person who removes ghosts from these people, right?" I smiled.

"You look like one," she replied, and I couldn't control myself. I laughed a lot. She too joined me. We both were sitting in my living room. There was total darkness in the house, and then there was laughter all around. She became the ray of light that I needed in my life. I finally found the reason for living. She was my little angel.

For two years, she visited me almost daily and became my treasured companion. Obviously, Randhir and Nandini, Randhir's first wife, were against her visiting me but Ahana somehow managed to come every day. She was full of joy and surprises. On a few days, she used to bring food for me as well. We used to talk a lot. She had so many questions about my profession, and I had so many stories of my granddaughter to share with her. Everything was just perfect.

It was her seventeenth birthday, and I was very excited about it. I had planned a surprise for her. I was waiting for her, but she didn't come at her usual time. I felt odd and restless, but she arrived soon after, though not in her usual happy mood. She appeared tense.

"What's the matter, Ahana? You seem to be a bit troubled. Is there anything I can help you with?" She started crying and I held her in my arms.

"I don't know why they just don't sort it out. Is it necessary to fight so loudly? I know they don't love each other, but why is it necessary to show it to everyone? Why can't they just pretend to be good parents? They should understand that they have a responsibility to handle." She stopped and cried again. I gave her a tissue. She left the sofa and went to see her reflection in the mirror on the opposite wall. She looked at herself as if she was looking at it for the first time. She adjusted her hair a bit and then took a long breath and continued, "Ahana couldn't sleep for the whole night. She was feeling afraid. She is not a strong girl. Her heart pounds so heavily when someone shouts in front of her. I somehow managed to console her."

I couldn't help but look at her in amazement. She was not Ahana. She was someone else.

"Is she still sleeping back at home?" I asked her while giving her a glass of water.

"Yes, I told her to stay in bed and not think too much about anything. She needs to relax. She is finding it all very difficult. Do you know how hard it is to console her? She never trusts anyone. She does like you, but she was not very fond of you. It was I who forced her to meet you. You are a good man. I saw you, and I told her to befriend you. Her faith lies only in me because I have saved her so many times," she said. She had a different kind of energy in her eyes. I was looking at her very closely. I had seen all this so many times but only in my patients. I had no idea that Ahana also had a personality within her. I was observing her very intently.

"I am glad that you felt good about me. I am grateful to you. But I have a question, why didn't you come to meet me earlier? We could have worked together for Ahana, right?"

"Ahana was not sure about it. She was not ready to let me go out of her. I did try to make her feel comfortable around me, but she is just a child. She feels afraid of everything, even me!" She chuckled. "She only allows me to talk when she is asleep. Finally, after years of cajoling her, today is the first day she let me go. She didn't want to miss out on meeting you on her birthday. She knew you must have been waiting, but she couldn't come. Her parents forced her to sleep in the room. That gave me a chance to convince her and here I am! You are the first person I have come to meet. But there's a secret..." she smiled looking at me.

"What?" I was curious.

"This is not the first time I am coming to meet you. I visited you earlier as well, but I came with Ahana, and that's why you didn't recognize me. Do you remember the time you played see-saw with me?" She was looking at me, waiting for me to recollect these experiences. "And the day when I fell asleep on your bed while you were telling me how you met your wife and the story of your marriage?"

Something struck me. I knew what was happening. I had never played with Ahana on the see-saw and never told her stories of my marriage. I was sure that this had never happened, but I had these memories with someone else.

"Yes, I remember now. You had fooled me, making me fall off the see-saw!" I took a step forward and gathered the courage to ask the question which would answer everything for me. "But you are yet to tell me your name. I can't call you Ahana, right?"

She paused. She was hesitant because she had never given a thought to naming her alter ego until now. Then she smiled and said her name for the very first time. "I am not Ahana. I am Jasmeen."

That was the last piece of the puzzle for me because Jasmeen was my granddaughter's name. I used to play see-saw with her. I used to tell her stories of my marriage when she used to sleep with me at night. I had narrated all these stories to Ahana about my granddaughter, and that had given birth to Jasmeen in Ahana. She was living the moments of my stories.

I should have felt anxious for Ahana, but I felt happy for myself. I had found Jasmeen, my Jasmeen. This was my secret. She was my secret.

Chapter 12
(Parveen)

"Let's try to work this out. Let's treat this as just another day in our life."

I took a long breath and looked at Randhir, who was sleeping on the sofa. We had had a fight the previous night, so he refused to come and sleep next to me. It was not an unusual thing in our home. We were used to these fights.

I silently left the bed and moved toward the kitchen to make tea for both of us. It took me ten minutes to make the 'strong' tea, just as Randhir likes it. I put the cups on a tray and placed them on the bedroom table and then woke Randhir up with a gentle shake. He left the sofa instantly and stretched himself. His muscles were aching because of the incorrect posture of his sleep. He said nothing, picked up the cup of tea, and started to drink. I did the same and sat next to him.

We silently finished the tea, and then I started to leave to take a bath because I was getting late for work, but Randhir stopped me.

"Where are you going?" he asked.

"To take a bath. I am getting late for work," I replied with a smile on my face.

"No need to go. Leave your job. I don't want you to work

for Digvijay," he said with no expression on his face. He was still sipping his tea.

"I think we have already had this conversation before. I can't leave the job. This is the only thing that brings bread to our home. You aren't earning anything, and..." I was cut short by Randhir's anger.

"Enough of this. You need money in the house; I'll bring it anyhow. But I just can't see you working for that asshole. He is the only reason that we are living like this. I am pretty sure that he was the one who made my boss believe that I was doing something fishy with the accounts of the company. He was the biggest client of my boss and he used his power to get me fired from my job, and he also made sure that I never got any other job. You do know how cunning he is. He goes to every possible extent to make things worse for his enemies," Randhir concluded his monologue.

"But why do you consider him your enemy? He just wants to treat your daughter. What is wrong with that?" I argued.

"He doesn't want to treat her. He is a fucking rapist. Didn't you hear Ahana? She wouldn't accuse anyone for no reason," Randhir replied as he approached me, fire in his eyes.

"You're losing your calm. I was there. The doctor clarified that it was just the result of the medication..." I started to say.

"SHUT UP!" Randhir interrupted, grabbing my neck and pressing me against the wall. "Shut the fuck up."

"Let me go." I struggled to speak. His grip was firm.

"Let me go, Randhir." I was choking and was about to lose consciousness when he came back to his senses and released me. I fell to the floor, and as soon as I regained my composure, I rushed to the bathroom. I made up my mind to leave the house without saying or listening to anything from Randhir.

When I reached Digvijay sir's house, the door was locked. I knew where the keys were, so I went to the guard room. The guard was sleeping, as usual. I looked inside the drawer and found the key. I rushed to the main door and unlocked it. The house was silent and smelt stale. Digvijay sir rarely visited as he spent most of his nights partying or at the office.

I went to the kitchen and prepared breakfast according to the instructions given to me by the doctor and Digvijay sir. When I finished, I went to the first floor and opened Ajay's room. I tried to be quiet because Ajay doesn't like to be disturbed. He was seventeen years old, chronically diabetic, thin, and bedridden due to a foot ulcer. He slept for almost twelve hours a day but always felt hungry, drank a lot of water, and urinated frequently.

I placed the food next to him and examined his feet. The wounds were oozing pus and blood. I took cotton and antiseptic to clean his wounds. While I was focused on his feet, I heard the television start with a loud noise. I was startled and was about to turn it off when I saw Ajay holding a PlayStation console and cursing at the television.

"It feels ticklish when you clean the wounds. Screw you, you son of a bitch!" He threw the console against the wall, shattering it. "There's another one in the cupboard. Get it for me."

I had learned to handle Ajay and made peace with his behaviour a long time ago. Many caretakers ran away because of his explosive nature, but I stayed because I had seen worse in my own home.

"Take this," I said as I gave him the console. "Here's your food. Please have it, and I have also kept your medicine..."

"Medicine? Do you think they help me? You're funny. Call them poison. They will help me die soon," he replied, laughing at his own joke. "Fuck you...fuck you..." He cursed at the television again.

I decided to leave him alone for a while and started walking towards the door when he called me.

"Hey, listen, whatever your name is, pass me that phone. I am fucking bored with these PS games. Let me check out the real stuff."

"Where is it?" I asked because I found nothing at the place where he was pointing.

"There…somewhere…I don't know where it is. Just look for it. It must be in the room only. Why the fuck are you here if you can't help me with things?"

I looked everywhere in the room but found no phone. I kept looking in each drawer and every corner, but it was nowhere to be found.

"I can't find it," I finally said.

"How would you find it? Can't you see it's in my hands? It was under my pillow. Okay, now go." He was glued to his phone. I wanted to slap him hard, but that wasn't possible. I was about to leave when he screamed in excitement.

"What the fuck? She is back. Awesome. How could this be possible? This is some deep shit. Awesome."

I left him screaming with his phone, closed the door behind me, and took a long breath of relief.

Chapter 13
(Ahana)

"I am sorry, love. But you are dead to the world," Digvijay said before leaving the room and closing the door behind him. As soon as he left, fear began to rise inside me. I hoped that Jasmeen would come to my rescue, and I felt like crying. Just as I was about to break down, a man rushed into the room carrying a gift-wrapped box. He placed the box in the centre of the room and quickly left without making eye contact.

I was scared of what to expect from the box. Should I open it or not? As I tried to figure out what to do, the box began to move. I almost screamed, wondering what could be inside it.

Suddenly, two men burst into the room and rushed towards me. One of them held my hands firmly while the other handcuffed me with a strange metal device. I tried to resist, but I was no match for them. Satisfied with their work, they left the room and locked me inside again, alone with the moving box.

I took a step forward towards the gift-wrapped box, not sure what I wanted to do. It continued to move vigorously, and I was really scared now. As I took a step back, an electric shock rushed down my spine, originating from the handcuffs. Someone wanted me to open the box, and if I refused or delayed, repeated electric shocks would be my punishment.

I screamed in pain and cried out, "What is it? Why are you doing this?"

Jasmeen took over and instructed me, "You want her to open the box? Alright, Ahana, do it."

"But I am afraid," I cried. "What if there are snakes or something else inside it? I just can't."

The electric shock ran through my body again, and this time I fell to the ground.

"She's doing it. Wait a minute, you fuckers," Jasmeen shouted. "Ahana, open it. I'm with you. Just open the damn thing and get it over with. There are no snakes in there. They don't want you to die. They're just playing with your fear. Don't be afraid of anything."

"Okay. Okay, wait. I'm doing it," I told Jasmeen and moved towards the box. As soon as I touched it, it started shaking again. I held it firmly and began tearing off the wrapping. I opened the box from above and threw it away with a scream. I caught a glimpse of what was inside. It was a dog. A brown-coloured street dog with its mouth sealed with tape.

"Calm down, Ahana."

"It's a dog. Oh my God. Please, take him away! Please... I'm afraid of dogs. Please... save me. Jasmeen, help me. Oh, somebody help me!" I was delirious with fear and started to scream and cry. Since childhood, the one thing I couldn't stand was a dog. I couldn't explain why I feared them. There was something that triggered inside me whenever I came in the vicinity of a dog. I lost all rational thought and became possessed by the fear of the unknown, and the same was happening to me now.

The dog appeared to be scared as well. It started running from one place to another. It wanted to rid itself of the tape on its mouth and was struggling with its feet. Finally, the dog succeeded and started to bark.

"Jasmeen! Where are you? Please do something. Jasmeen..." I screamed, and the dog continued barking at me. We were both scared of each other.

It took us some time to get to our comfort zones at the two farthest corners of the room. The dog stopped barking, and I stopped crying. Our eyes were on each other, but suddenly the dog fell to the ground and started to whimper.

"He's hungry," Jasmeen said.

I didn't reply. My eyes were still on the dog.

"What should I do now?" I asked Jasmeen.

"You can't do anything. Just wait for them to do something. We're just puppets to them," Jasmeen replied.

"I want to go home." I cried.

"There's no home for us."

"I hope somehow my dad comes to meet me. I'll convince him to take me back home. He can turn things around like he did the last time." I knew it wasn't possible now, but I needed some positivity.

"For him, you are not even alive, I guess. Sooner or later, he'll accept the fact that you are no more. The police will stop looking for you, and that bitch, your stepmother, will convince your father to stop searching for you." Jasmeen paused for a moment before continuing, "There's only one man who can help. He's the only one who knows that you're in danger: Mahesh uncle." Jasmeen concluded.

Chapter 14
(Mahesh)

I thought about it one more time before getting out of the car, which I had been driving for the last half hour to reach my destination. I looked at the sign that read 'Police Station', took a deep breath, and stepped out of the car. Nervously, I walked towards the stairs that led me to the table where the station in charge, Lakhan Srivastava, was writing something in a file.

"Sir?" I said, and he signalled me to sit down. He didn't lift his head; otherwise, he would have recognized me. He was the inspector who had taken me into custody when Digvijay had accused me of being a paedophile. I remembered that night I had spent with the inspector clearly in my head. It was a nightmare. I'm sure he remembered it as well.

I sat down on the chair opposite him, sweating because I had no idea what the outcome of my visit would be. The visuals of that night were coming back to haunt me, but I had to do this for Jasmeen. She was in danger, and maybe I was the only one who knew the facts.

Finally, the inspector lifted his head and looked me in the eye. He recognized me instantly and leaned back on his chair with a mischievous smile on his face. "Mr Mahesh, the psychiatrist. How are you? It's been a long time since you visited." His smile had a hint of mischief. I took out a handkerchief from my pocket and wiped my face.

"Yeah, it's too hot here. I have urged the government so many times to install some ACs here, but you know, no one cares about us." The inspector looked at me for a few seconds and continued, "So? Tell me, Mr Mahesh, how can I help you?"

"I heard that you are about to close Ahana's case?" I asked in almost a whisper.

"Maybe. But who told you that?" The inspector arched his eyebrows.

"I think I have some information that could help you with the case."

"What kind of information?" He straightened himself in his chair. He knew about the relationship between me and Randhir and how invested I was in this case. He was aware that I was the source of most of the leaks that came up in the media, which is why he knew I was telling the truth. I could have something useful.

"Can I have a pen, please?" I asked, and he obliged without taking his eyes off me. "And a piece of paper, please." He was getting annoyed and visibly frustrated, but he gave me the paper.

I wrote the eleven-digit number on the paper and handed it to the inspector. He had no idea what it was. He looked at me in utter confusion, but before he could say anything, I clarified, "It's an account number. It belonged to Ahana."

"Why is it significant? How could it be helpful to us?" The inspector handed the number to one of his constables, who pulled up bank records on a computer to get the details while the inspector kept his focus on me.

"It was active throughout the days of her disappearance. Ahana used it every day. Through this account, she kept me informed about her whereabouts. But for the last four days, it has not been used. She's in some danger." I said teary-eyed.

"Why didn't you tell us about this earlier? Was Randhir involved in this as well? Is there anyone other than you who knew where Ahana was? You're in deep danger now, Mr Mahesh, so I want you to confess everything you know, right now!" He screamed at me.

"I'm sorry, inspector. She... Jasmeen... I mean Ahana. Oh, fuck I'm sorry. I did it to save her from her parents... I'm sorry." I started to break under the pressure.

The inspector leaned forward and took my collar in his hands, warning me with his finger. "Start talking, or else. You do know how much I love you. I'm sure you still remember the last meeting we had in this place."

"Yes sir, wait... I'm telling you everything. It was the day when..." I drifted back to the memory of the day when I saw Ahana for the last time.

It was the time when I usually took a walk in the neighbourhood after having my dinner. That day, I was very happy about something. I have no recollection of what it was, but that was why I was later than my usual time. It was about midnight, and I was roaming around with an empty mind when I heard a thud near the window of Randhir's house. Instantly, I was on guard. I waited for something to move, but nothing happened.

I waited for a few more seconds and then called out, "Who's there?" No response. I thought it must be a cat or something, but I needed to be sure.

I moved towards the sound and called out again, "Who's there?" This time, I almost shouted, and when I was not expecting any response, I got one.

"It's me, and please don't shout. They will hear you." It was Ahana. She had a big trolley bag with her and a backpack.

"What are you doing? Where are you going?" I got agitated

because I knew the answer to my questions. She was running away.

"I am running away, and I request you not to stop me." Ahana seemed to be in a hurry.

"Okay, I get it that you are running away, but where to and why? What happened to you?" I tried to argue.

"Don't you know what happened to me? Does anyone care what happened to me in that hospital where they want to send me again? That bitch is doing drama and saying that I am trying to kill her! Why the hell would I try to kill her? Who the hell is she?" It was Jasmeen who was talking to me. I could tell by the gestures she was making. "They never asked me about the rape thing, and do you know why? Because they think that it was the worst thing that happened to me, but they have no fucking idea what Ahana and I actually faced there every fucking day."

"Relax, Jasmeen. Come to my house first. Let's sit and have a cup of coffee, and then we'll talk everything out. It is not safe for Ahana out there. We need to talk about this first for the safety of Ahana." I consoled Jasmeen, and she nodded. I knew how sensitive she was for Ahana, and that is what I had to use.

The inspector interrupted my thoughts and asked, "Your granddaughter's name is also Jasmeen, right? Is there anything that you find strange here?"

"The patients of Multiple Personality Disorder often take names and references of the places and persons that are around them. It is always in their subconscious. Maybe there was some story that fascinated her about Jasmeen and she took the name from there." I tried to answer confidently so the inspector couldn't read my bluff. He nodded.

I continued…

Chapter 15
(Ahana)

I could hear my stomach making strange noises; I was hungry. The dog was also trying to sleep as it was feeling the wrath of hunger inside him, too. We were both comfortable with each other now.

There was no movement in the room, everything was quiet when suddenly I heard footsteps outside. Someone or something was coming.

The gate opened, and another box arrived. This time, I did not hesitate to open the box. Even the dog was excited to see what was inside the box, or maybe he smelled the contents and that made him jump.

I opened the box with anticipation, and when my eyes fell on the contents, I left the box on the ground and sat in a far corner of the room. The box was not for me but for the dog; it had food for him. The dog merrily ate the food, and while chewing, he looked me in the eye a few times as if inviting me to join him. But it was dog food, and I just couldn't eat it. I felt like crying. I looked at the CCTV that was watching me 24/7, hoping that someone would feel sympathetic and send some food for me as well.

I watched the dog eat the food until it licked everything off the box, and once done, went back to its place at the far corner and sat down. Its eyes were still fixed on me.

Minutes turned into hours, and now I knew that something was not right. Something was happening or was about to happen. My food would not arrive. Strange thoughts were crossing my mind. I looked at the dog. It was shaking its head strangely while sleeping. The shaking turned more violent. It woke up and started making very scary noises.

The thought that had just crossed my mind vanished into thin air as the violent growls and barks of the dog filled me with fear. The dog's eyes now glowed with rage, and I realized that something in the food had turned him mad.

"Jasmeen? What's happening? What should I do?" I asked, but there was no answer. The dog was now on its feet, growling and barking ferociously. Its sharp teeth and intense stance made me back away, wanting to retreat as far as possible, even to the point of entering the wall.

"Jasmeen, help me...somebody, please help me!" I shouted, but the dog leapt at me. I grabbed it by the neck and continued shouting, with it just inches away from my face, barking like a maniac. Suddenly my fear disappeared, replaced by a need to defend myself. Strength took over my fear.

Suddenly, the gate opened again, and a knife appeared in the room. I knew what they wanted me to do, and this time, I wanted the same thing. I threw the dog away, jumped over the knife, and sliced open the dog's stomach as it charged at me once again. The dog cried out in pain, blood spilling all over. I continued to stare into its eyes with no remorse as if I was showing it the power I possessed. I kept stabbing the dog for a while, my mind blank. I don't know when two men entered the room with food and took everything away. I was no longer hungry, but I still ate to gather the strength I would need for whatever they had planned for me next.

Chapter 16
(Mahesh)

I gave her some coffee, and we sat across from each other on the sofa while sipping it. My eyes were fixed on her leg, which was tapping restlessly against the floor. Jasmeen was full of anger, and that drove Ahana far away from her own body. Jasmeen had completely taken over Ahana. I saw the rhythm of her leg's tap break for a moment and took that as an opportunity to breach her anger.

"How's the coffee?" I asked her.

"Does it matter? Does it really matter to you? You are worried about the coffee? What about me? I was running from here, from you, from everyone here, and you care about the coffee?" Jasmeen shouted, targeting her anger at me. She threw the cup away, and it shattered just a few inches from my feet.

I placed the mug of coffee on the table that I had in my hand and rushed to grab her. She cried. I gave her my shoulder. I had no idea what had triggered her so badly.

"That bitch, she first killed her own husband, and now, now she wants to get rid of me so that she can live with Ahana's father in peace. She thinks Ahana is the only hindrance left in her life and she wants her to rot in that mental hospital. She doesn't care about anything. Those fuckers planned everything. That Randhir

and Parveen, they are both murderers," she blabbered.

I kept running my hand through her hair to console her. I was not able to hear what she was saying. She must have been talking rubbish because, in anger, we say such things. So, I knew the first and foremost thing required was to give her warmth and comfort before she could think clearly. She kept crying and blabbering simultaneously. After a while, she was only sobbing. I lifted her head and looked into her eyes.

"I love you, Jasmeen. I hope you know that," I said to her.

"I love you too."

Inspector Lakhan interrupted me again.

"Wait a minute. Why is this Jasmeen so fond of you?" He was visibly confused.

"I don't know. The stories that such patients weave around themselves are always too difficult to comprehend. Maybe she saw me as a friend, a guardian, or maybe her own grandfather as she named herself Jasmeen. I have no idea."

"Okay. Continue."

"I'll always be there for you. You don't need to run from anyone. I am here to protect you always," I said, trying to give her strength, but she seemed distant.

"You can't always be there to protect me. Inside those walls, I'm on my own. Ahana is just a child. She needs protection, and I'm there for her. But when I need someone to lean on, there's no one. You can't be there for me," Jasmeen argued.

There was silence between us for a while, and then she told me what had triggered her.

"Just a few hours ago, she staged it as if I was going to kill her. She made Randhir believe that I'm unstable. Can you believe it? Can I do such a thing? Tomorrow they'll call the hospital people and ask them to take Ahana back to that hell. Should I

wait for that moment, or should I do something about it right now? Ahana can't handle that barbarian treatment. I had to take action."

"But Randhir won't allow such a thing, will he? He loves you, right?"

"Randhir? He does love Ahana, but he loves Parveen more. There are things that you don't know about Randhir. Ahana knows, but she doesn't believe her eyes. I don't know if I should tell you because Ahana doesn't want me to tell anyone about this." Jasmeen was confused.

"You can tell me. There's no secret between us, right? You do know I'm always on your side. Ahana can trust me. She does trust me."

"Ahana was there when...when her mother jumped off the roof. She saw everything. She was on the stairs or somewhere around there and she saw everything. It wasn't a jump. There was a man there, standing just behind Ahana's mother. She thinks... Well, I think as well, that it was Randhir who pushed her off the roof, and that's because he wanted Parveen in his life. I've seen that murderous look in both their eyes. They both have something strange about them. They're both capable of doing horrible things."

"This can't be true. Randhir...he loved his wife. I've seen how he almost worshipped her."

"That's the problem. Everyone only looks at the picture that's being portrayed to them, but no one is ready to look beyond it. Just tell me, if Randhir worshipped her so much, why would she commit suicide? Was there any reason for it? And why would Ahana say such a thing, that she saw it happen in front of her eyes?"

"Ahana saw everything? Are you sure that is what she said?" The inspector interrupted again.

"That is exactly what she said."

The inspector was lost in his thoughts trying to connect the dots. I was looking at him when he said, "Carry on with the story. Why have you stopped?"

"I just can't live with them and give them Ahana on a platter to do whatever they want. Ahana is too vulnerable in front of them. I can't take that risk. I have to run away from them," Jasmeen said, determined.

I wanted to stop her, but I did not know how. My mind was overwhelmed with so many options at once, and I couldn't process anything.

"I... You can't just...okay, listen to me. Where will you go?" I finally asked, trying to be practical.

"I don't know. I haven't thought of anything," Jasmeen replied flatly.

"Wait a minute. Let me think of something. Give me a few days to think, and then—"

"Days? They will bring the hospital people tomorrow to my home, and then I'll be imprisoned inside those walls of that fucking hospital, where I'll be tortured until death. I can't wait for even an hour. If they find out that I am not in the house and have tried to escape, they will do everything in their power to find me and send me back to hell," Jasmeen said, getting more agitated.

"But...what about me? How will I...you just can't abandon me. I can't live like this. At least give me a few minutes to think," I said, feeling helpless.

I got frustrated and ran towards the window from where I could see Randhir's house. I was looking at it blankly when an idea came to my mind.

"Okay, listen to me. You need to go to Delhi. Meet my friend's daughter there. Her name is Kiran. I'll ask my friend to

arrange everything for you. They will help you enrol in college for your studies. No one will suspect anything, and I'll make sure of it. You just need to stay in touch with me."

"If I'll be in touch with you, don't you think they will get to me through you? Don't be so naïve," Jasmeen responded, feeling sceptical.

"You don't need to call me every day. You just need to use this account number every day." I gave her a piece of paper on which I had written all the details of the account number. "You just need to use this account every day, and I'll get to know your location and everything. This will help me know that you are doing fine. Promise me that you'll do this for me. You may need money as well, and this will help. I want you to enjoy your new life, but I also don't want you to forget me because... because... you do know what you mean to me..." I choked on my words and felt tears roll down my cheeks.

Jasmeen looked at me with no expression on her face. She waited for a while and then hugged me, took the piece of paper on which I had written the details, and left.

"That was the last day I saw her." I had tears in my eyes.

"I still don't know why you are so attached to her," the Inspector said and then called someone and instructed them to leave for Delhi and inquire at the college. He then asked another constable to ask for Randhir to come to the station.

"You can go for now, Mahesh, but don't leave the city. We may call you soon." He said this and got back to work.

I left the station wiping my tears away.

Chapter 17
(Randhir)

I could hear a low humming sound coming from the other room, disturbing my sleep. There was something unsettling in the atmosphere that I couldn't quite put my finger on. Although I tried to get up from the bed, my body was unresponsive. I strained to listen to the low humming to try to understand it better.

"You need to sleep, Rani. Stop playing around. I need to sleep, and you need to sleep. We both need to sleep... Hmmmm... Hmm..." It was Nandini's voice, talking to Ahana, our daughter. I focused on her voice, trying to make sense of it. "You can't drive me insane, Rani. You won't like it... Hmm... Hmm... Don't you like my smiling face? Haven't you noticed I've stopped smiling since your birth... Hmm... Hmm..." She was talking and singing in a strange, low tone.

I wanted to go to the other room, but my body wouldn't budge. Beads of sweat were running down my forehead.

"You spoiled everything for me. You took every happiness from my life... Hmmmm... Hmm... Do I deserve this? I brought you into this world, and you are paying me back like this? Hmm... Hmm..." Her voice broke a little, and she began to cry.

Suddenly, the humming stopped, and her voice went silent. It felt like I was running in a corridor. The corridor looked familiar, like the one in the hospital where Nandini had given birth to Ahana. I ran like a maniac, knowing exactly where I had to go–the operation theatre. There was no one in the corridor or at the entrance to the OT. I rushed inside and slammed the door ajar, seeing Nandini on the bed in front of me. There were no doctors around. I stayed there glued to the spot for a while, watching as Nandini held Ahana in her arms, covered in blood.

"She isn't breathing. I tried to save her, but she isn't breathing. I think she's dead," Nandini said, smiling. She had killed my Ahana.

I woke up feeling disoriented. The dream had felt so real that I was panting. Parveen woke up on hearing my rushed breaths and brought me some water. I emptied the glass instantly and asked for more. I was sweating heavily.

"What happened? Was it the dream again?" Parveen asked.

I nodded. This was not the first time I woke up in this state. She rubbed my back, and we both stayed silent until I felt normal.

I then checked my phone for the time and saw that it was seven in the morning. I wondered why the alarm hadn't gone off and then realized it was Sunday. I smiled to myself, realizing it didn't matter what day of the week it was.

Parveen got out of bed and went to the kitchen to make tea for us when my phone rang. It was Inspector Lakhan Srivastava. My heart started beating rapidly. What could be the news? It was early in the morning on a Sunday.

"Yes?" I picked up the phone and responded.

"Please come to the station. We need to talk about something," he said in an unemotional voice.

"What is it about, sir? Did you find something?" I asked out of curiosity.

"I need you to come here, and then we'll talk in detail," he said before ending the call.

Parveen rushed over and asked, "What is it?"

"I don't know. They're calling me to the station," I replied without thinking.

"But what's the matter?" she asked again.

"I don't know," I shouted at her. "Will you please shut up now?"

It was a long, tense drive to the police station with various scary thoughts running through my mind. When I finally reached the station, I wasted no time and went straight to Lakhan Srivastava's office. He was eating samosas when I arrived and instructed me to sit on the opposite chair. He then called someone to take away the samosas, wiped his hands with tissues, and sat upright, looking deep into my eyes.

"Mr Randhir," he said, taking a long pause. "Do you know why we have called you here?"

"You never told me, sir," I replied.

"Any guess?" He tried to be comical, which annoyed me, but I kept my calm.

"I... I don't know, sir."

"So sad." He took another pause and continued, "We have two pieces of news for you. One is good and one is bad. Which one would you like to hear first?"

"The good one," I said hesitantly.

"We have something new on Ahana. A lead to search for her whereabouts." My eyes lit up with joy. I didn't care about the bad news. I smiled and had no idea what to say. "And now comes the bad news. We may find Ahana soon."

"What's bad in it? I don't understand."

"How innocent. You are a good actor, Mr Randhir."

"Sorry...I don't understand."

"We know what happened to your wife. We have an eyewitness

statement, and once we find Ahana, we'll have the eyewitness as well. You won't be able to run away again, Mr Randhir." His gaze was fixed on me. I got furious and stood up from the chair.

"What do you mean? What are you getting at? The death of my wife was because of suicide. She committed suicide, and it is in your records. Why are you blaming me all of a sudden?" I was shouting, and all eyes were on me now.

"Anger," he said, taking a pause and coming forward to put one of his hands on my shoulder. "Do you know, Mr Randhir, that anger is the first refuge of a liar? Call a thief, a thief and their first reaction would be anger. The same goes for a murderer." He whispered the last word in my ear.

"You are just incompetent people. You can't find a missing girl, and to beat around the bush, you're simply picking things up from the past to deflect the questions that the media will ask. I'll expose you people." I walked out of the police station muttering under my breath. The inspector sat back in his chair and started to smile. I heard him shout behind me.

"Oye, bring those samosas back. I am fucking hungry. I need to go out as well to catch some murderers around."

Chapter 18
(Parveen)

"What the fuck are you doing?" Ajay exclaimed as soon as I touched his feet to apply the medicine.

"What?" I asked, irritated. It was his time to sleep but I don't know what engaged him so deeply on his phone that he lay awake. He was continuously watching something on it.

"Not talking to you," he replied.

I went back to my work. It was almost seven in the evening and I had to finish my work here and go back home. I was eager to know what happened at the police station. Randhir was not answering my calls, and I was worried, but this bastard was making my job tough and it irritated the hell out of me.

"Don't you have to sleep now?" I finally asked.

"I am not feeling sleepy. Why? What is your business in it? You want to steal something from the house? Well, go ahead. I don't fucking care." He said in his usual disrespectful manner.

"You have no sense to talk to your elders, right?" my anger suddenly burst out and accidentally I punctured one of the blisters on his feet. It started to bleed, and that made everything messy.

"What the fuck is your problem? You are just my nurse. Don't be my mother. And please be a little careful! It hurts, you fucking bitch. You do know I can get you replaced anytime. I'm sure you don't want your family to suffer because I know about your financial state, bitch." He snapped at me and brought me back to reality. I just couldn't say anything to him. I had to bear whatever he threw at me because I needed him, and not the other way round.

"Be still at least." I grabbed his leg when he tried to move away.

"What is it? What is it?" Ajay got excited.

"Nothing just..." Then I realized he was not talking to me but to his phone again.

"Oh! Shit...fuck...kill him! God damn it... Kill the dog..."

I was getting irritated with all this shouting and movements and hastened my work. I was about to go out of the room when he screamed again.

"She killed the dog. Woah!"

I turned for a moment and then shook my head in disbelief.

"Is this funny for you? Killing and all?" I asked him.

"Not funny...but...you don't know what I am watching. You don't have any idea," he replied.

"What? A drama series? Movie? What is it?"

"A reality show." He kept the phone aside and for the first time, he looked me in my eyes and asked, "Okay, tell me. What will you choose? Your own sanity or a dog's life?"

"What?"

"Yes, tell me. Consider yourself trapped in a room with a mad dog. If you don't kill it, it'll kill you. What will you choose in such circumstances?"

"If you don't obey my instructions or if you try to tell anyone about my intentions, you'll lose this job and probably, you'll not have anything to feed your family ever. You do know what I can do. Right?"

"What happened?" he asked again. "Difficult, isn't it?"

"I will kill the dog," I replied.

He smiled. "It is always easy to kill the dog."

We both kept staring at each other for a while. It seemed as if we were communicating something. Suddenly I felt like withdrawing my eyes so I did and turned back and closed the door behind me. I left the house and took an auto to return home. Throughout the journey back home, I recalled that instance when I had chosen to kill the 'dog'.

"There are few things that I have discovered about Ahana that can harm your family's image if it comes out in public," Digvijay called me into his cabin and asked me to sit in front of him as he wanted to discuss something important.

"I don't understand, sir."

"How much do you love Ahana?" Digvijay asked an abrupt question.

"I love her as a daughter, sir."

"But she is not your own daughter. Okay, tell me, how much do you love Randhir?"

"What happened, sir? What do you want to ask?"

"If I make you choose one out of Ahana and Randhir, whom will you choose?"

"Why would I choose?"

"Because I asked you to."

"It is difficult for me." I was sweating.

"Nandini didn't fall on her own. She was pushed." His words landed on me like a bullet. "And I think you already know that. But you are unaware of who pushed her."

I stayed silent. I took the glass of water and drank it. "Randhir wasn't the one who pushed her. Ahana told me that story as well. Jasmeen made her believe that Randhir had pushed..."

"Exactly. You are right. Jasmeen made Ahana believe that it

was Randhir who pushed Nandini from the roof that night but it was not Randhir who did it."

There was a pause and after that Digvijay said, "It was Ahana herself who did it."

"Why would Ahana do something like that? Why?"

"That doesn't matter as of now. The thing that matters is that I have confessions of both, Ahana and Jasmeen. I can accuse Ahana and Randhir both of the murder. Now tell me, who would you like to save?"

I was clueless because in both cases I would lose Randhir forever. He loved Ahana a lot. He could kill himself for Ahana. I was feeling short of breath.

"Or...or you can help me with something that I want," Digvijay suggested the third option to me.

"What? I'll do it. Tell me."

"What if you choose to save two lives in exchange for one?" he left his seat and came behind my chair to say the words, "Kill Ajay for me."

Chapter 19
(Mahesh)

"We're still trying to find out what happened, but please focus on your life and don't worry about me. I think it's time for you to move on. If you keep looking for..." I was interrupted by a knock on the door. "Listen, I'm hanging up now. Someone's at the door." I disconnected the call and walked towards the door. Peeking through the door, I was shocked to find Randhir.

I took a deep breath before opening the door. As soon as I did, I was ready to fight because I knew what his visit was about. However, Randhir came inside silently and sat on the chair. I closed the door and sat next to him. We stayed there, without uttering a single word for a couple of minutes before Randhir broke the silence.

"Do you know what the police are talking about?"

I was not aware of what he was asking. I was not aware of how much he knew or what the police had told him. However, I took a gamble and hid my involvement in the findings. "They told me they found something in Delhi. Maybe they have proof that Ahana is living in Delhi, but she escaped silently before the police reached her, and now she is in some danger. I don't know the details." I waited to see his reaction. For a while, he sat there with empty eyes and then he started crying.

"She's in danger now? Wasn't she in danger before? Was she enjoying out there?" He continued crying, and I tried to console him. "What did they tell you?" I asked him.

"They want to reopen Nandini's case. They say that Ahana is running from us because I murdered her mother, and now Parveen wants to hurt her. She is afraid of us, and that's why she's running from us. Can you believe that? It is absurd! She loved me. She loves me. I know that."

"Have faith in God, Randhir. She'll come back soon."

"She won't! The police are not trying to find her. They want to lock me up. They're just working as agents for Digvijay. It's all his plan to steal my daughter from me. I think, I think...he already has my daughter with him, and the police are helping him keep the matter subdued so that the media doesn't get excited about the case. They just want to reopen Nandini's case so that people forget Ahana's accusations against Digvijay's hospital."

"Should we ask Digvijay?" I was naïve to suggest it, but I had nothing else to offer.

"And what would I ask him?"

"About Ahana's whereabouts?"

"And he'll talk like a parrot, you think?"

"What if we drop all charges against Digvijay? Will he leave us alone and return our Ahana?" I asked, using 'our' for Ahana for the first time. Randhir noticed but said nothing. He knew how much I loved Ahana. He thought for a moment before breaking the silence.

"Do you know anyone in the media who can help us?" he asked.

"Yes. I have connections," I said.

Randhir nodded and paced back and forth in the room. I could see he was nervous. He didn't want to make the call, but our love for Ahana was stronger than anything in this world.

"Hello?" The call was answered, and Randhir stopped pacing.

"Listen to me. I know you have Ahana with you. The police are helping you. You are a powerful man and can influence everything, but my stature is not the same as yours. I am just a father who loves his daughter and is ready to do anything for her. I am ready to come in front of the media and take all the blame for Ahana's accusations against your hospital. I beg you to return my daughter. Please call me back." He ended the call.

"He didn't pick up?" I asked.

"No. I left an audio message for him. Let's hope he responds. But what if he knows nothing about Ahana? What then?" Randhir asked, voicing the same fear I had.

"That's not possible. He must know something. I'm sure of it." I bluffed. We had nothing left to do but wait.

Chapter 20

The inspector was asleep, and it was five in the morning. The police station was quiet, and the only sound anyone could hear was the snoring of the inspector.

"Wake up. Are you the thana-in-charge? O bhau!" Inspector Pulkit, sent by Lakhan Srivastava, tried to wake him up.

"Who is it?" The thana-in-charge finally woke up and yawned with one of his eyes closed.

"We have come from Meerut. You must have heard about our arrival. We are here to inquire about Ahana–Ahana Tyagi." Inspector Pulkit shared some official papers by placing them on the table.

"Oh yes. Please have a seat. Oye chhotu, bring some tea for the sahab log." He shouted and then gestured for us to grab the opposite chair, "Please have a seat."

"Thank you. I am in a bit of a hurry, so if you can please start by telling me what you have found..."

"Yes, sure. The thing is, there is no girl as per your description at the college who goes by the name of Ahana. But... But there is one whose name is Jasmeen, and I guess she is the one you are looking for. I inquired at the college and got to know that all her papers were forged. The college where she was studying is not a very reputable kind of college. They just need students to fill up the seats, and that's why they don't bother about the papers and such formalities."

"Yes, Jasmeen is the one we are looking for. Actually, the girl is suffering from..." Inspector Pulkit tried to explain but was interrupted in between.

"I know...I researched about it as well. She is suffering from MPD, the kind of disease we see in movies... *Aparichit*... what a great movie... Vikram did a fantastic job. I was so scared after watching the movie." The thana-in-charge started to laugh sheepishly.

"So, where is she now? This Jasmeen. Have you asked the college about her friends and all..." Inspector Pulkit tried to bring the topic back on track.

"We have completed our investigation, sir. Don't worry, we have statements from everyone at the college, but unfortunately, we don't have the girl with us. She ran away before we could reach her."

"No leads or anything? Where can we look? Any best friend or anything like that? Love angle...anything that can help us find her?" Inspector Pulkit was getting anxious.

"Sorry, sir. We have nothing like that, but I have one thing to tell you. We arrested her on one occasion."

"Arrested? Why?"

"She was found at a rave party, completely soaked in drugs with her friends. We took everyone and put them behind bars for one night and released them all the next day. Her friends confirm that since that night, she hasn't returned to college. She fled and simply vanished into thin air."

"And no one complained about it? No missing report from any of her friends? Or did you file any case against her that night? Anything like that?"

"Sir ji, they are college students. They do things for fun. If we file a report, their lives will be ruined. We don't want them to suffer. We simply keep them locked up for one night and release them the next day. And about the missing case, it happened just a few days ago. Let me check." He checked a few files and then confirmed, "Yes, it happened five days ago. Her friends didn't even notice that she wasn't with them."

Pulkit became restless and wanted to leave.

"Arre sir, at least have some tea," the thana-in-charge called, but Pulkit was long gone. He came out and called Lakhan Srivastava.

He told Lakhan everything he had found about Ahana. Lakhan listened in silence and then cut the call. It was another dead end in Ahana's case.

Chapter 21
(Digvijay)

"Listen to me once. I know you have Ahana with you. The police are helping you out. You are a big man and can have influence over everything, but my stature is not the same as yours. I am just a father who loves his daughter, and for her, I am ready to do anything. I am ready to come in front of the media and take all the blame for Ahana's accusations against your hospital. I beg you to return my daughter. Please call me back." I heard the audio message, and it felt really good.

"She is making good money for us, but how long should we carry on with this? We can't keep her forever. We need to think about something. The police can connect the dots anytime and reach us." Daisy, my secretary who handled my 'other' businesses, was briefing me about the money we were making through Ahana.

Ahana was a very good find for us, but we got to know her value quite late. We first tried to sell her organs as we usually do with the patients we can manage. 'Managing' meant we could keep such patients in our facility practically forever because even their families were not interested in them. No parent wants to have their child back unless they are completely cured. But we miscalculated the love Randhir had for Ahana. We could have landed in trouble, but the organ-selling procedure didn't work at all. She was a misfit. Her organs were not that perfect.

We then tried to make money through various other endeavours where rich people came to fulfil their desires with the bodies of young girls, but it was not sufficient for us. And then came the idea where we hit the jackpot. Daisy was the one who came up with the idea of using Jasmeen to make more money. The idea was to use the dark web.

Well, to explain the dark web, think of the Internet as one iceberg. The ten per cent above the water is what we usually see and use – like your Google and social media and all the stuff you browse through your browser. But there is a deeper ninety per cent called the deep web. Within that deep web, a small, hidden area exists called the dark web. The dark web operates differently from the regular Internet. It uses special technology called TOR – which stands for The Onion Router. Tor routes your Internet connection through a network of servers around the world, so nobody can trace it back to you. This basically means you have anonymity which you don't have on the surface web. Once you're in there – you'll find a different kind of Internet.

We took the dark web to another level and created a kind of reality show that people saw and gambled on. Jasmeen became an instant hit. People loved to see her reactions to various situations, and because of her spontaneity and feisty spirit, people loved to gamble on the outcomes of such situations. But then Randhir took our golden bird away from us. That spoilt everything for us. No other face, no other activity worked. We had to bring Ahana back, anyhow, and finally, the police themselves brought our jackpot back to us.

"The police will never connect the dots because they are being managed," I replied to Daisy. She was not aware that I had paid a lot of money to keep the police officials quiet about Ahana's disappearance from her college. Everything was planned. But risks were always present because we were dealing with the dark web. Anything and everything was doubtful here.

"Even if that is the case, you are right. We can't do this forever. We need to find a solution to make the money we want in a single go, and I think I have that solution in my mind," I continued.

"What is it, sir?" asked Daisy.

"You need not know right now. I'll tell you everything soon. We'll be debt-free very soon," I smiled.

"You mean we can make four hundred crores? Is that possible?" Daisy was surprised.

"Four hundred crores or maybe even more," I replied, looking at the email I had received the day before. It held the ticket to my victory.

"That means you need not worry about Ajay anymore?" Daisy asked the question that had been bothering me for years.

"Yes, Daisy. But that doesn't mean he'll live. He needs to die. "The money doesn't belong to him. It is mine." I didn't realize it, but the last line came out much louder than I had intended. I was angry, and whenever I was reminded of the injustice, the anger flowed automatically out of me.

I still remember the day when my elder brother made his son the legal heir of our business. He had already lost his wife when Ajay came to this world. I knew from that moment that this Ajay would prove to be a demon for our family and the same happened. Ajay was only four years old when his father announced his will. My brother was dying, and instead of giving the business to me, he made me just the guardian of the property for his son, Ajay. I was to handle the business only until Ajay reached the age of eighteen, and also, I had no power to make any decisions on my own. There were a number of directors who would first approve everything. I was not the owner; I was just a guardian. That made me hate Ajay, and that hatred was visible on my face.

Daisy left the cabin. She knew I wanted to be alone. I looked at the email again.

"You...yes, you will change everything for me. I just need to be careful. Mr Lover boy."

Chapter 22
(Parag)

I remember seeing you sitting alone in that park, playing with your hair and talking to someone who wasn't there. I decided to approach you, taking each step cautiously and looking around, but I was sure that you were alone. I sat down next to you on the park bench without introducing myself. You stopped talking immediately and looked afraid. I felt the same way, but I wanted you to feel safe around me. I wasn't here to scare you, I was just in love with you.

"Hey," I said, trying to initiate conversation.

"Hi," you replied in a funny voice that I found cute.

"I saw you talking to someone, but I couldn't see anyone around. I thought I'd come and chat with you. Is that okay?" I said, looking around.

"I don't talk to strangers. My father is about to come. You should leave," you replied directly.

"Okay. But can I give you a gift as a token of the friendship we just started?"

"We're not friends yet."

"But we will be someday. What's the gift?"

"Here it is." I gave you your favourite chocolate, and you snatched it from my hand and started to eat it.

"Do you like it?" I asked.

"I love it. You can stay here as long as you want. My father isn't coming, and my mother won't mind you," you smiled.

That smile is still fresh in my heart, even after all this time. I wish I could see it again, but how? How can you smile without me? You feel alone, but you don't even know that I'm watching you 24/7. I keep my eyes open until they hurt just to witness every breath you take. You have no idea how much I love you. You have no idea what I would do to see that smile on your face again. 'Jasmeen' doesn't suit you at all. You are Ahana, and I want you to always remember that.

> *Don't cry, Ahana. It's not your fault. It was Jasmeen who made you do all this. You're not a monster like her. You're pure like an angel.*

I commented on the live feed, hoping my words would reach you somehow. I was hurt to see you killing and crying over the live feed, and I wanted to touch you, to console you, but how? I felt so helpless. I cried while looking at you on my smartphone when I received the email that changed everything for me.

"Ahana, I will come for you. Don't worry."

Chapter 23
(Parag)

I sat in my room, lost in thought. I had spent the entire night replaying the video, and my thoughts kept returning to Ahana. I loved her dearly – her beautiful face, her kind and gentle spirit, and her captivating smile – all of which were permanently etched in my memory.

I tried to shake these thoughts away and focus on something else, but my mind was still drawn to her. I had known her since childhood, and now, after so many years, she was a captive on the dark web. I could not fathom how this had happened to her and didn't know what I could do to save her.

I got up and paced the room, waiting for a response to the email I had sent to the person who had uploaded the video. I did not know what to expect, but I was willing to do anything to save Ahana. I had already offered them money and my own life, but they had not shown interest…I guess that wasn't enough for them.

In desperation, I closed my eyes and spoke aloud, "If only I could give them something else, something more valuable than money or my own life. Something they could never get from anyone else..."

I had never felt so helpless and powerless. I wanted to do

something to help her but was not sure what. I had been trying to think of a plan, but my mind drew a blank each time. I also needed to think of keeping my reputation intact so I couldn't talk about this openly.

My thoughts kept returning to her. I looked out of the window at the moonlit night and took a deep breath, trying to clear my mind and think of anything that could help her.

I knew I had to save her, no matter the cost. I walked to my desk and opened my laptop to research the dark web for any information that could help me. I knew it would be a difficult journey, but I was determined to find a way to save Ahana.

I examined every webpage carefully, cautious not to get caught in any traps. As a politician, I had access to many resources that could help me get to the bottom of this racket and identify the perpetrators. I knew the dark web was delicate, but I was ready to do whatever it took to bring Ahana home safely.

I worked late into the night, searching for any information that might help me save Ahana—but nothing helpful showed up. I needed to wait for the captors' response; other than that, I could do nothing.

When I was almost tired of waiting, I finally received an email. It read:

> *Dear Parag,*
> *We have received your email, and we appreciate your concern for Ahana. We are willing to negotiate her release, but it will come at a price. We want you to use your political power to get us something, and in exchange, we will release Ahana unharmed. Now you must be wondering about the 'something' part. Well, that's not very difficult for you. You must already know about the hundred-acre land near*

Pragati Vihar phase 3 that comes under forest land. We simply want you to declare it commercial. If you do not comply, we will ensure that Ahana will always be in front of your eyes, but only through the dark web.

Think carefully about your decision, Parag. You have one week to respond.

Sincerely,
The Captors

My hands trembled as I read the email. I couldn't believe what I was reading. I had to make a decision that could affect both mine and Ahana's life forever.

I knew complying with their demands meant breaking the law. The land that the captors were asking for was in the news because of me. I was the one who had taken the decision to stand against the government's decision to sell the forest-reserved land to nearby hospitals and for other commercial activities. But I also knew that I couldn't let Ahana suffer any longer. I had to do something to save her.

I took a deep breath and began to think. I had to devise a plan to get Ahana out. I thought about it for hours, going through every possible scenario in my head. I didn't even realize when I fell asleep with the thoughts of Ahana in my mind.

I dreamt of Ahana sitting on a bench in the park. I approached her and asked, "Are you okay?"

Ahana nodded, but her eyes were sad.

"What's wrong?" I asked.

Ahana hesitated before speaking. "I don't think I can survive this, Parag. I feel so helpless, so vulnerable. I can't take it anymore."

I put my arm around her shoulders. "Don't worry, Ahana. I won't let anything happen to you. I promise."

Suddenly, the scene changed, and I found myself in a dark alleyway. I heard Ahana's screams and ran towards her voice. When I reached her, I saw her being dragged away by a man with a knife.

My heart raced as I thought of a way to save her. I knew I had to act fast but didn't know what to do.

I quickly assessed the situation and saw that the man was not paying attention to me. I took advantage of the man's distraction and kicked him in the groin, causing him to drop the knife.

I quickly grabbed the knife and pointed it at the man. "Let her go," I said, my voice shaking. I started stabbing the man in the same way that I had seen Ahana stabbing the dog in the video. It was merciless; it was cruel, but it was needed.

I woke up from my dream abruptly. I was sweating heavily. I went up to the window again, took a deep breath, and realized that I knew what to do now.

Chapter 24
(Ahana)

I was alone in the room, observing the walls and my environment with a careful eye. I was being watched constantly, I knew, by the ever-present eyes of the CCTV camera that was perched like a bird of prey in the corner of the room. I could feel its gaze on me, and the knowledge that I was being monitored sent a chill down my spine.

The room was the same as I had left it – stark and bare, nothing but the four walls that surrounded me like a prison. The only thing that was breaking the monotony of the dull grey walls was a single fly buzzing and flitting around me incessantly as if it were mocking me.

My patience was wearing thin. I wanted nothing more than to catch the fly and squash it between my fingers until it was nothing but a lifeless and mangled mess. The thought of taking its life filled me with a feeling of power as if I was the ruler of this domain and I wanted to savour that feeling.

I had already tried every method I could think of to catch the fly, but none of them had worked. I jumped up and down trying to reach it by stretching my arms as high as I could. I threw my pillow at it. I even tried making a buzzing sound imitating a fly thinking that it would somehow notice that and come towards me. I would kill it with my bare hands then. But it continued buzzing around absolutely oblivious of my tricks.

I was determined to catch it, no matter what. I had the feeling that capturing and killing the fly would give me some measure of control over my own life, however small that may be.

Finally, after hours of trying, I managed to catch the fly. It had landed on my arm, and I had quickly swatted it down, trapping it between my hands. Its little legs were still twitching, and at that moment, I felt a sense of triumph wash over me. I had done it. I had killed the fly.

I couldn't help the broad, feral grin that spread across my face. I was filled with a feeling of immense power. I had conquered the fly and felt like I had conquered a part of me too. I let out a wild laugh, a wild, maniacal laugh that echoed off the walls and filled the air around me. I looked at the CCTV camera and knew it had seen my triumph.

But I wasn't ashamed. I felt powerful, and I liked it. This was my moment, and I was going to savour it.

Digvijay was getting excited behind the camera in the control room while watching Ahana. His fingers tapped restlessly against his thigh, the sound of a muted drumbeat in the otherwise silent control room. As Ahana's maniacal laughter rang through the giant television screen, 78,000 viewers were tuned in with rapt attention — an absolutely remarkable feat, considering there had been no prior notification about this fly encounter. He couldn't stop staring at her, transfixed by the sheer charm and energy radiating from her. How could anyone not be drawn to her?

Digvijay sighed and shook his head as if Jasmeen was in front of him and he was talking to her. "I wish I didn't have to let you go, but we both know that to reach somewhere in life, you must move away from one place."

He looked at the screen where Parag was participating in the discussion on the issue of the forest land in the parliament.

"Today, I stand before you to talk about the importance

of hospitals and the need for more of them. As we all know, healthcare is a fundamental right of all citizens and essential to the functioning of our society. While forests are also important, we cannot ignore the pressing need for more hospitals.

"Thousands of lives are saved or improved daily due to quality healthcare provided by our hospitals. The availability of necessary medical equipment and personnel and the support of experienced medical staff are essential to providing quality life-saving care. Unfortunately, far too many of our citizens cannot access such care due to a lack of adequate facilities.

"I know I decided to stand against the government's plan of turning Pragati Vihar Phase 3 into a commercial area, but after talking to people and seeing their needs, I realized I was wrong. I want to apologize for my previous position, and now I want to correct things by supporting the government in building more hospitals in Pragati Vihar. At the same time, we can continue to increase our forest cover by planting more trees."

While the discussion was taking place, Digvijay's phone started to buzz. He picked it up knowing who could have called. It was Jhunjhunwala, the most significant player in the investing market, who was to benefit from the development of Pragati Vihar.

"I don't know how you did it, and I don't even want to know. I just want to let you know that you did a great job. I'll send the promised amount to your account soon. It was a pleasure doing business with you." Jhunjhunwala abruptly ended the call, leaving Digvijay with a feeling of accomplishment. With a triumphant grin stretching across his face, he turned his gaze towards the television, where Ahana had her unrelenting eyes fixed on him. The intensity of her gaze sent shivers down his spine as if she could see right through him and into his soul. "My precious!" he murmured under his breath.

Chapter 25
(Parveen)

I adjusted the sheets around him, taking a moment to look into Ajay's eyes. I had an inexplicable feeling that his eyes held a secret that I should uncover. He was only fifteen, but his body had suffered enough for many lifetimes.

He had spent the past few months in a lot of pain, his diabetes steadily getting out of control and his body deteriorating. He had been diagnosed two years ago, and it had already taken a heavy toll. His skin had lost its sheen, his eyes had lost their spark, and his posture had become unbearably slumped.

I had seen Ajay's erratic behaviour. I had seen his anger and pain, but it wasn't until now that I truly understood the full spectrum of his struggle. He was, in a word, broken.

"Fuck! Fuck! Fuck! What the fuck is she trying to do?" Ajay shouted excitedly. I was startled by the sudden sound in the silent room. I looked in Ajay's direction. He was sleeping a moment before and was sitting upright now on the bed staring into his mobile.

"She is becoming a killer!" He screamed.

I did not pay any attention to him. I turned my back and continued to clean his bloody foot trying to ignore his moans. He was so engrossed in his phone that he did not even glance at me as I disinfected and dressed the wound.

"This is getting worse. I think we need to call the doctor for this." I was talking to myself, as I had assumed Ajay was not listening to me. But this time, he was. He actually responded to me.

"Why bother? Just give me some of that medicine and leave me be. Either way, I'm not going to be here for very long." Ajay responded, but I could see something in his eyes. Part of me felt guilty because I was the cause of his discomfort. Another part of me wondered if he understood what was happening to him and if his response was a recognition that I had something to do with it.

An eerie silence hung in the air until Ajay's sharp shout of joy pierced it. His gaze was fixed on his phone screen, and he cried gleefully, "She did it! The girl finally killed it." His laughter was wild and uncontrolled as he added, "She's so unpredictable."

I was now curious and could no longer resist asking, "What is it that excites you? Is it a video game or a web series?" I really wanted to know what was it that kept him engrossed so deeply.

"Not at all. These things don't excite me anymore. This is real-life shit. This girl is rocking the dark web." Ajay seemed to be in a good mood today. He was responding to my questions which was a rare event. I took the liberty as well and kept throwing more questions.

"Real-life shit on mobile? I don't understand."

"This girl is being held captive in a room, her life depending on how she deals with crazy tasks and death-defying assignments. It's like nothing I've ever seen before!" His voice grew more profound as his leg slammed onto the bed, sending jolts of pain coursing through him. He grinned wickedly, his eyes glinting menacingly like a deranged lunatic, determined to watch this show of survival until the end.

I couldn't believe what I was hearing. Was this girl being held captive and forced to do dangerous tasks for someone's twisted amusement? It made my skin crawl just thinking about it. But Ajay seemed to revel in it. It was as if he was living vicariously through her.

"What kind of tasks are we talking about here?" I asked cautiously, not sure if I wanted to know the answer.

"Oh, they're pretty intense. Do you remember the dog thing that we discussed? It was from this show only. She decided to kill the dog, and it was fucking awesome. Almost all the games challenge the psychology of this girl, and she excels in almost everything. She is fucking insane." Ajay's eyes shone with excitement as he recounted the events.

I felt sick to my stomach. This was not the type of thing that should be celebrated or enjoyed. I wondered what kind of person Ajay was to find pleasure in someone else's suffering.

"You know, it's not right to enjoy someone else's pain and suffering," I finally spoke up. "That girl is in a terrible situation, and we should be doing something to help her, not watching her for entertainment."

Ajay's grin faltered momentarily before he shrugged and said, "It's not like we can do anything to help her. And besides, she signed up for this."

"What do you mean she signed up for this?"

"I mean, she must have signed for it, right? She must be getting paid or something. I don't know..." For the first time, I saw Ajay in doubt. He started to feel awkward about my question. He had never thought about it before.

"But you said she's a captive?"

"Uh, well. She must be. I don't know, and I don't care," Ajay replied.

He returned to the video, but I couldn't help being intrigued by what I had discovered. Should I risk trying to learn more? Ajay's temper was volatile, and anything could set him off.

"Do you know the girl you are watching on your phone? I mean, is she any heroine or something?" I tried to keep the conversation going but got no response from Ajay.

Ajay didn't want to engage in further conversation with me, and I couldn't blame him. His words had left me feeling disgusted, unable to process the notion that people could actually find entertainment in the suffering of others. It was a concept that struck me as incredibly pathetic and morally bankrupt.

I tried hard, but my mind was still revolving around the girl. The pain and suffering of innocent individuals are exploited for the amusement of others. It was a cruel dance, a perverse masquerade I wanted no part of, but something still made me restless.

I took a deep breath, hoping to clear my mind and regain my composure. Perhaps, I thought, the world had always been this way, and I was only now opening my eyes to its harsh realities.

I did my duties with renewed determination, checking his blood sugar levels, administering medication, and ensuring his comfort. The rhythmic beeping of machines and the hushed whispers of the night staff, which included two servants and a cook, provided a backdrop to our silent vigil.

As I carefully adjusted the machines around Ajay, his sudden movement caused his mobile phone to slip from his grasp. It clattered to the ground, and before I could react, his pent-up frustration erupted in a burst of anger.

"What the hell? Can't you do anything right?" Ajay's voice trembled with a mixture of pain and rage. His outburst caught me off guard, and my initial instinct was to defend myself.

"I…wait…it was…" But I quickly realized that this wasn't the time or place for a confrontation.

Taking a deep breath, I suppressed my impatience and tried to maintain a calm tone. "Your sudden movement caused it to slip...wait...let me...."

"Oh please, now don't teach me and grab my fucking phone. They are about to announce something important." Ajay shouted.

I tiptoed around the medical equipment, reaching under his bed to retrieve the fallen device. It seemed to have slipped quite far away, requiring me to stretch further than I had anticipated. Determined, I finally grasped the phone and pulled it out from its hiding place.

As I prepared to hand it back to Ajay, my eyes inadvertently glanced at the screen. My heart thumped painfully in my chest as I saw what he was watching, and my throat was constricted with shock. There was no mistaking who it was; that girl we had just been talking about – it was Ahana, our Ahana!

A million questions raced through my mind, but before I could even begin to comprehend what was happening, I felt a wave of dread wash over me at the thought of what this might mean.

Ajay's anger seemed to dissipate as he noticed my reaction. He bit his lower lip, and his brow creased, creating a series of tiny wrinkles that splayed outward from the corners of his eyes like an asterisk. "What's wrong? Why do you look like you've seen a ghost?"

Chapter 26
(Randhir)

I was sitting all alone in my room; the pale orange light of sunset seeping in through the closed blinds and giving the space an eerie glow. My heart thumped nervously inside my chest as I stared at my phone, waiting for it to buzz with the information I desperately sought. I had spent months searching for answers and yet all I had gained was more confusion and doubt. Finally, I had taken the step which I had never dreamt of before.

Suddenly, my phone began to vibrate on the desk in front of me. I looked at the caller ID and my heart started beating faster. It was Digvijay – the man who had emerged as my arch-enemy. I was expecting this call but still looking at his name flashing on my phone's screen made me behave erratically.

"Hello," I said, my voice heavy with trepidation.

"I loved your message. It took me time to respond because, you know, I am a busy person." He paused and then said the words that I had been waiting to hear, "I know where your daughter is." His tone was cold and calculating.

I felt my entire body go cold. I had been searching for my daughter for years with no luck, and here he was, telling me he had the answer. I knew that it wasn't going to be easy – nothing ever was when it came to Digvijay.

"What do you want in exchange?" I asked, my voice quavering slightly.

"I want you to admit that you were wrong about me and my hospital. The same thing that you promised to do in your message," he said. "I want you to confess your mistake in front of the press."

My heart ached at the thought of having to make such a public confession, but I knew I had no choice. This was my daughter we were talking about – her safety and well-being were all that mattered.

"Alright," I said, my voice barely above a whisper. "I'll do it."

"Good," he said. "I'll wait to see your face on television. Don't disappoint me."

And then he hung up.

I sat in my chair, motionless, as the realization of what I had just done sunk in. I had been falsely accused and now I was being asked to admit my mistake in order to find my daughter. I felt a wave of despair wash over me as I thought of the long journey ahead of me. But I knew it was my only hope of finding her, and I was determined to follow through with it.

I took a deep breath and picked up my phone again. This time, I dialled Tanmay's number.

"Hello, Tanmay?" I said as soon as he picked up. "This is Randhir. Mahesh gave me your number."

"Ah, yes. How can I help you, Randhir?" Tanmay asked. "Wait a minute. Your name is ringing some bells in my head. Wait a second...oh, yes, you are Ahana's father, right? Tell me how can I help you?" His voice suddenly felt more enthusiastic than before.

"I need your help. I need to make a public confession in front of the press," I said, my voice shaking slightly.

"Why? What happened?" Tanmay asked. He was confused now.

"I can't tell you over the phone. Can we meet in person to discuss this?" I asked.

"Sure. When and where do you want to meet?" Tanmay asked.

"Tomorrow, at 10 a.m. My place. Please bring your camera. You will need to record and maybe telecast later."

"Okay, I'll see you there at 10 a.m. tomorrow," Tanmay said before hanging up.

I sat back in my chair and took a deep breath. The next few days were going to be tough, but I had to do whatever it took to find my daughter. I knew that Digvijay was not to be trusted, but I had no other option. I would have to trust him, at least for now.

The next morning, Tanmay arrived promptly at 10 and we sat down on the sofa in the living room. He had brought a cameraman with him who adjusted the camera and waited for Tanmay to signal him to start recording.

"So, what's going on, Randhir?" Tanmay asked, looking at me expectantly.

"I need your help to make a public confession," I said, taking a deep breath.

Tanmay raised his eyebrows in surprise. "A public confession? About what?"

I hesitated for a moment before finally speaking. "I accused Divya Hospital of doing something terrible, but I was wrong. They were actually helping my daughter, Ahana, with her treatment. The doses were high, and it made her say some strange things, but I took them seriously and accused the hospital of selling her organs and other things. I was completely wrong, and I need to make it right."

Tanmay nodded slowly, his expression serious. "You do know that it will change everything in Ahana's case? That's a pretty serious thing that you are about to say. Are you sure you want to go public with this?"

I nodded firmly. "I have to. I need to clear their name and make things right. I know I made a mistake, but I'm willing to make up for it." I could not tell everything to Tanmay. There were things that only I could know.

Tanmay looked at me for a moment before nodding. "Okay, we'll do it. But remember, once this is out there, there's no taking it back. Are you sure you're ready for the consequences?"

I took a deep breath and nodded. "I'm sure. I have to do this."

Tanmay signalled his cameraman to start recording and turned back to me. "Okay, Randhir. Whenever you're ready."

I took a deep breath and began to speak. "I would like to make a public confession. I accused Divya Hospital of some terrible things, but I was wrong. They were actually helping my daughter with her treatment, and I took their actions out of context. I'm sorry for any harm I may have caused and I hope that this confession can help clear their name and reputation. I know my mistake may have caused irreparable damage, but I'm willing to take responsibility for my actions and make up for them in any way possible."

As I continued to speak, I could feel the weight of my words on my shoulders. It was as if the entire world was listening to me, judging me for my mistakes. But I knew that this was something that I had to do. After I finished speaking, there was a moment of silence as Tanmay and the cameraman processed what I had just said. Then, Tanmay turned to the camera and spoke. "You just heard it, folks, a public confession from Randhir, the man who made some serious allegations against Divya Hospital. However, as he just revealed, he was wrong. We hope this confession can help clear the air and Divya Hospital can move on from this controversy."

I felt a sense of relief wash over me as Tanmay wrapped up the recording. I knew my actions had consequences but was willing to face them head-on.

I wanted to relax for a moment, but a knock on my door startled me. I thought it was Parveen returning home from her late night shift at Digvijay's house. She told me that she would be staying there for the whole night because Ajay needed some more medication.

I went to open the door and when I did, I was surprised to see a tall, muscular man standing before me. He was wearing a khaki uniform. I wondered what a policeman was doing here at this hour and how fast the news of my confession had spread. "Mr Randhir?" he asked, his voice deep and serious.

"Yes, that's me," I replied, feeling a sense of unease creeping up on me.

"I am here to arrest you on the charges of your wife's murder," he said.

Without waiting for my response, he grabbed my hand and took me towards his jeep.

Tanmay came running behind. His cameraman followed him. Everything was getting recorded, so the police officer wanted it to be quick. He pushed me into the jeep, and as I was being rushed away, I saw Parveen running towards us. She was clueless about what just happened. I was clueless as well.

Chapter 27

The police station looked the same as expected. The paint was peeling from its walls, the windows were cracked and the roof was in need of repair. The austere brick building stood out in stark contrast to the surrounding landscape. The dark windows gave off a haunting feeling as if the spirits of the past still lingered here. Inside was a single room with a long wooden desk, several chairs, and bookshelves full of tribal records. In the corner of the room was a large, old safe with ancient locks.

Inspector Lakhan sat on his chair, his hands gripping the handles tightly. His heart raced faster as he felt the intense scrutiny of Tanmay, observing every move of his. He knew that the reporter was here to ask him questions about the arrest of Randhir, and Lakhan was not sure how to answer them. He had been cautious to ensure that the investigation details were kept secret so as not to let news of the arrest get out and invite questions from the public. But he was unfortunate. Tanmay was already present at Randhir's house at the time of the arrest and was the first one to notice and record everything. Lakhan was sure that he must have recorded the arrest as well. There was no use hiding anything; still, he had to be sure not to leak too much information.

Tanmay must have sensed Lakhan's unease, for he said, "Inspector, I'm sure you know why I am here. Why don't you start by telling me the grounds on which you have arrested Randhir? Can you tell me what evidence you have?"

Lakhan sighed in resignation. He knew he had to answer the reporter's questions; otherwise, he would be in for a lot of trouble. He had seen the damage a negative story could do to a person's reputation, and he didn't want to be the subject of such a story himself. His promotion was due in a few days and if anything went haywire, he would lose the opportunity. He cleared his throat before speaking.

"What's your interest in the case? Why are you asking? How do you know Randhir?" Lakhan decided to launch the offensive.

"I am a friend of the family. My interest is because of one of your failed endeavours, sir. You must know about the lost daughter of the family. If you are not ready to speak about Randhir, we can talk about the daughter as well."

"We had received a video of Randhir's daughter, Ahana, where she confessed to seeing her father push her mother off the roof," he admitted. "That is the evidence we have."

Tanmay frowned. "If you had this video, why didn't you search for Ahana herself? Why didn't you follow that lead to find her?"

Lakhan was at a loss for words. He knew that if he was unable to give a convincing answer, the reporter would be sure to include it in his article. He had to think of something to say quickly.

"Well," he said, trying to come up with an excuse, "we were busy with other cases and there is only so much we can do. Besides, we had the video, and it was all we needed to make the arrest."

Tanmay nodded, seemingly accepting this explanation. Lakhan breathed a sigh of relief. He knew he had managed to dodge a bullet this time, but he had to make sure it didn't happen again. He had to come up with a better excuse next time, or else his reputation would be ruined.

"From where did you get the video?" Tanmay asked.

"From anonymous sources. We are investigating that as well," Lakhan replied nonchalantly.

As they were talking, Tanmay's phone rang. He looked at the screen and saw that it was Mahesh. He excused himself from Lakhan and answered the phone.

"Hello, Mahesh. What is it? I am at the police station..." Tanmay was interrupted by Mahesh.

"Tanmay, I need you to come to my house right now. It's important," Mahesh said urgently.

"What's going on? Can't you tell me over the phone? I am trying to drill inspector Lakhan about the arrest of..." Tanmay was again cut short by Mahesh.

"No, I can't. It's something I need to tell you in person. It's about Ahana," Mahesh said, his voice urgent and fearful.

Tanmay hesitated. He didn't like the sound of Mahesh's tone. It sounded like something serious was going on. But he also didn't want to leave Lakhan.

"Okay, Mahesh. I am on my way."

Tanmay hung up and looked at Lakhan apologetically. "I have to go. It's an emergency," he said.

Lakhan nodded, understanding the gravity of the situation. "Go ahead. Duty calls, I understand. We can continue this conversation later." Lakhan was relieved, but he didn't show it on his face.

Tanmay left the police station and got into his car. As he started driving towards Mahesh's house, his mind was in turmoil. He couldn't help but think about the recent events; everything was happening so fast. First Randhir's call for confession about the hospital, then the arrest of Randhir on the charges of his first wife's murder and now news of Ahana from Mahesh.

He pressed down on the accelerator, trying to get to Mahesh's house as quickly as possible. He could feel his heart pounding in his chest and sweating profusely. He didn't know what to expect, but he knew it wasn't good.

Finally, he reached Mahesh's house and parked his car outside. He got out and ran towards the door, his mind racing with all sorts of terrible scenarios. When he reached the door, he found it was already open. He pushed it gently and entered the house.

The first thing he noticed was the presence of Parveen. Her eyes were all red because of excessive crying. *But why was she here? With Mahesh?*

"Mahesh, what's going on? Where's Ahana?" Tanmay asked, his voice trembling. "What do you want to tell?"

Mahesh looked at him, his face grim. "It's about Ahana. Parveen told me about her and since then I am really worried about her..."

Mahesh couldn't even finish his sentence when Parveen was overwhelmed by her emotions yet again and cried uncontrollably. After much cajoling she stopped and started to speak, her voice choked with emotion, "Last night, I was with Ajay, Digvijay's son. When I was working there, Ajay was watching something on his phone. It was a show, and we casually started to talk about it. There was a girl trapped in a room doing various kinds of activities for the sake of entertainment of people. I didn't understand any of it but then my eyes fell on the video. The girl... that girl who was trapped was Ahana. It was a deeply disturbing video of Ahana. She was being kept in a room, and a strange reality show was happening with her as the protagonist. I didn't understand it at first, but then I realized it belonged to something called the dark web."

Tanmay's blood ran cold. He felt a wave of nausea wash over him. "The dark web? What kind of sick people could do something like that? And how is this possible?" Mahesh spoke up. "I did some digging after Parveen told me about it. It turns out that some people run these kinds of shows on the dark web. They capture innocent people and force them to do unspeakable things, all for the entertainment of morally depleted individuals who pay to watch."

Tanmay felt sick to his stomach. "Since how long has this been going on? And how did she reach there?"

Mahesh replied, "I have been trying to find out more about this show but it is difficult to get any information about it. I've been trying to track down the source of the video but failed miserably. The dark web is a vast and dangerous place. Maybe you can use your sources and get some insights?"

Tanmay looked at Parveen, who was still weeping uncontrollably. He put a hand on her shoulder and tried to comfort her. "We'll find her, Parveen. I'll try my best."

Parveen gasped in shock as she remembered that she had seen Tanmay at the scene when her husband was arrested. She enquired, "Were you at the police station earlier? What was happening? What charges have been brought against Randhir?"

Tanmay took a moment to make sense of all that had happened since morning. Where was all this leading them? What was the story? He replied, "They are accusing Randhir of murdering his ex-wife. A video has surfaced with Ahana's confession that she saw him push Nandini off the roof that fateful night."

"This can't be true! How can they say that without any basis? Where did they get such evidence?" Mahesh was confused. This is what Jasmeen had told him when she met him for the last time. How did the police get this information? He was feeling both angry and helpless.

"Anonymous sources, they say," Tanmay sighed hopelessly, "I'm so confused now between who is right and who is wrong. With this dark web stuff involved, I'm beginning to suspect Digvijay may have something to do with it."

"That rascal is definitely involved. He knows everything. Don't you see the timing of everything? First, he makes Randhir confess about the hospital and then releases the video of Ahana and gives it to the police to get him arrested." Mahesh paced the room like a caged animal in frustration and in the heat of the moment, he said the thing that was not supposed to be said in front of Tanmay. "Digvijay was the one who made Randhir say those things about the hospital!"

Does that mean none of that was true? Why would you do this? What were you thinking?" Tanmay lost his temper now. He was being polite all the way along but now he couldn't control his anger.

"He promised to give us the whereabouts of Ahana and we thought this was the only way to get to her. Shit...how stupid of us to trust that villain." Mahesh sat down on the sofa and felt like a lost man. Everything seemed to be slipping from his hand yet again.

All of us sat there, disappointed, and then Parveen asked the most important thing.

"What should we do now?"

Chapter 28
(Digvijay)

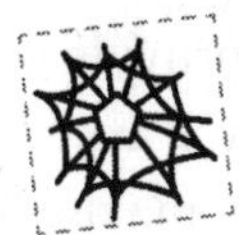

It took numerous attempts, but I succeeded eventually. After so many unsuccessful attempts, I finally regained that which was rightfully mine—fame and fortune. I knew Jhunjhunwala well, and I understood what he desired—a piece of land. I had disappointed him on multiple occasions in the past before my luck changed dramatically. It must have been God's way of rewarding me for my good deeds from previous births. He had taken smaller joys away from me only to give me even bigger things in life later. Thanks to Parag's email, I obtained four hundred crore rupees with a single stroke.

Now it was time to fulfil another promise, one that was more difficult than the first. I sat at my workstation and opened the mail from Parag.

I am writing to you to remind you of the agreement we made concerning Ahana. As you know, I have done exactly what I promised and have successfully had the land in question changed from forest land to commercial land.

However, now it is your turn to fulfil your end of the bargain. You promised that you would return Ahana to me safe and sound after the work is done. I have done my part, but you are yet to fulfil yours. I am waiting for your reply.

I couldn't help but chuckle at his request. He thought the world revolved around his whims and wishes! How naïve could people be! Love truly makes people blind!

Sighing, I began to draft my response to the mail. I didn't want our esteemed politician to wait any longer.

"We are making arrangements for it. It will take about a week's time before we can provide an update."

I wasn't quite sure why I asked for a week's time; perhaps I needed more money, or maybe I had developed a strange attraction towards Ahana...erm, Jasmeen. Regardless of what it was, I knew I had enough time as Parag was unable to do anything now. His career was in shambles and while that may have been an end of sorts for him, there were still many things ahead for me.

My phone suddenly began to buzz, and I saw Mahesh's name flashing on the screen. With a smile, I answered the call.

"Hello, Mahesh. How are you?" I asked cheerfully.

"I know it was your plan all along to send that video to the police," Mahesh said angrily. "You still have Ahana, and I swear..."

I didn't want to listen to his tirade, so I quickly interrupted him.

"If you already know everything, why are you wasting my time? Just go to the police and tell them what happened—maybe they'll come to arrest me." My good mood wasn't going to be spoiled by him.

"Karma will get you in the end," Mahesh spat before I cut him off again.

"I'll wait for it," I said before hanging up.

As I moved away from the laptop, another email caught my eye. It had been lying in my inbox for some time now and the sender's name looked familiar but I couldn't place where I had seen it before. Intrigued, I opened the email and read:

I can give you what you always wanted, Mr Digvijay—if you give me Ahana.

Another admirer of Ahana? A strange fear pulsed through me as my eyes darted over the message, and I realized what truly scared me—how did the sender know my name? My mind reeled as I wondered who on earth could be aware that I was her captor.

I got restless. I had to find out who this person was. I had to know from where he got the information that I had anything to do with Ahana's disappearance.

I replied to the email promptly,

All that is great but who are you?

The reply came almost immediately.

The one who knows you better than anyone else.

Chapter 29
(Tanmay)

The bus was packed, and I had to squeeze my way through the crowd to find an empty seat. I could feel the eyes of the other passengers on me as if they knew I was on a mission. But I kept my composure and managed to secure a seat in the back corner, away from their prying glances.

Finally, I had a moment to myself. Glancing out the window at the passing scenery, I noticed the sun setting, casting a soft orange hue on the landscape. The warm air carried the countryside's pleasant smells, and I felt at peace for the first time in the last few hours.

Just then the thoughts of Ahana flooded my mind, and despair washed over me. I was determined to find her, but I needed a starting point. I recalled Mahesh's words – the last known location of Ahana was a college in Delhi. I had to find out what happened to her.

I took out my phone and started researching more about the college where Ahana was studying before her disappearance. I needed more information about the college and the people who might be involved in Ahana's case.

Making a mental note, I decided to call my contacts in Delhi and ask around, hoping someone knew something about Ahana or the college. Saving her from this darkness became my sole purpose. I also needed to keep in touch with my colleagues who were assisting Parveen to get Randhir out of jail. I had already found a lawyer for them and was doing my best to support their cause.

Shifting in my seat, I felt a newfound determination. I would find Ahana, and I would ensure her safety.

As I disembarked from the bus, I took a deep breath and surveyed my surroundings. I was in the heart of Delhi, surrounded by people and buildings. The city's energy pulsed through me, urging me forward. I pulled out my phone and typed in the name of the college Mahesh had provided. It was only a few blocks away, and I started walking towards it with purpose in my stride.

As I approached the campus, the sounds of students laughing and talking filled the air. It made me feel a twinge of sadness as I thought about Ahana, who was once a part of this vibrant community. Showing Ahana's picture to a few groups of students, I soon got to know about Kiran, who was a friend of Ahana, as the students informed me. Now, I knew I had to find Kiran, hoping she could provide some information about Ahana's last known whereabouts.

I walked through the college, making my way towards the administration building. Outside, a group of students were gathered, laughing and joking, unaware of the pain I was feeling. I approached them and showed them Ahana's photograph.

"This is Ahana. She used to study here. I'm trying to find out where she is now. Someone mentioned that there's a girl named Kiran who knows Ahana. Do any of you know Kiran from the Computer Science department, second year?"

The group of students exchanged uncertain glances, clearly hesitant to respond. I could sense fear in their eyes, knowing that they were hiding something. Undeterred, I persisted, determined to get the information I needed.

"Please, it's serious. I need to talk to Kiran about Ahana," I said, my voice firm and unwavering.

Finally, one of the students spoke up. "I know Kiran. She's in her class."

Relief washed over me as I felt like I was finally making progress. I followed the student to a classroom on the second floor, my heart beating rapidly in my chest. I couldn't help but wonder what I would discover about Ahana and her sudden disappearance.

As I entered the classroom with Kiran sitting in the last row, her surprise was clear when she looked up from her notebook, her long hair framing her face. The other student left us alone, and I knew this was my chance to get some answers about Ahana.

Taking a deep breath, I approached Kiran's desk and showed her the photograph. I could immediately sense her uneasiness.

Kiran's eyes widened with recognition as she gazed at the picture of Ahana. Memories of the party flooded back, and fear coursed through her veins. She knew I was seeking answers, but she seemed unsure if she could provide them.

"I haven't seen Ahana in a while," Kiran whispered, her voice barely audible.

"I know that. That's why I'm here, to ask you what happened. What's the last thing you remember about Ahana?" I inquired, trying to be gentle yet insistent.

Kiran's eyes darted around the room as if searching for an escape. She didn't want to relive that terrible night, but she knew she couldn't stay silent any longer.

"I was with Ahana at the party. We were drinking and having a good time when the police showed up," Kiran started, her voice trembling.

"Police?" I was taken aback.

"They accused Ahana of taking drugs and took her away

with them. I tried to stop them, but they wouldn't listen. I never saw Ahana again after that."

Listening closely, I figured that Ahana's disappearance was more complicated than I had anticipated.

"Did the police say where they were taking her?" I asked, hoping for a hint.

Kiran shook her head. "No, they didn't. They just took her away, leaving us all in shock."

The feeling of helplessness was coming back, but I knew I couldn't give up on finding Ahana. My determination grew stronger as I continued to question Kiran.

"Did anyone else see where the police took her?" I asked.

Kiran looked down at her notebook, her hands trembling slightly. "I don't know. I was too scared to look."

Sighing, I ran my hand through my hair, feeling the weight of frustration. I thanked Kiran for her time and left the classroom, determined to follow any lead I could find about Ahana's disappearance. As I walked down the hallway, I couldn't shake the feeling that this was just the beginning of a long and challenging journey.

As I entered the police station, tension gripped me. My heart pounded in my chest as I approached the front desk, where a constable was dealing with another lady who was there to file a report. Although he was misbehaving, I decided to bite my tongue this time, refraining from speaking out as my priority was to extract information.

"I am here to inquire about a raid that took place on 26 June, when the police arrested a girl named Ahana. I want to speak to the officer who handled the case," I stated directly.

The constable responded with sarcasm, asking, "Who are you? James Bond?" Nevertheless, I showed him my ID, revealing that I was a journalist.

"So, why do you bother about it? Do you have any permission for this inquiry?" he asked, seemingly dismissive.

Maintaining my composure, I responded firmly, "Listen, I have access to information that you wouldn't want to deal with. I know people who can make things difficult for you in your job. Let's cooperate here, or I can call Gupta ji, and he can handle things for me if you prefer." The mention of Gupta ji was a bluff, but I spoke with enough confidence to convince the constable.

He paused and eyed me suspiciously before relenting eventually. "No need to bother Gupta ji. We are here to help but we need to confirm the intentions, right? Everyone here thinks that we are here only to argue. Wait, I will take you to the officer."

The constable and I reached the cabin of the officer who seemed busy with paperwork. I took a seat, trying to maintain a calm and polite demeanour as I broached the sensitive topic.

"Sir, I am here to inquire about an incident that occurred on 26 June at a pub, where a girl named Ahana was reportedly arrested. Can you provide me with any information regarding that?" I asked, trying to be respectful.

The officer looked up, a hint of annoyance clear in his expression, "I'm not aware of any such incident. Do we have any records of this?" He asked the constable.

"No sir. Not in my knowledge." the constable responded. The best part of the whole scenario was that both of them didn't even think about looking through the records as if they knew every record by heart.

I knew this was going to be a challenging conversation. I decided to play the bluff, hoping it might lead to some useful information. "Sir, I understand that records may sometimes be missing or incomplete. However, the pub has CCTV cameras, and we managed to obtain the footage from that night. It clearly shows the police taking Ahana away. I was hoping to get some clarity in this matter."

The officer's expression changed, and he leaned forward, looking more attentive now. "CCTV footage, you say? How did you manage to get that?"

"I have my ways, sir," I replied cryptically, keeping up the façade.

The officer seemed to consider his next move carefully. "Well, even if there was an incident, we might not have filed a formal arrest report. It could have been a minor issue that got resolved at the station."

"But what happened after that? Where is Ahana now?" I pressed, feigning concern.

The officer sighed, realizing that I wasn't going to back down easily. "Alright, let me check some unofficial records. Sometimes, such incidents are off the books. But don't expect me to reveal too much."

He started going through some papers, and I pretended to wait patiently. After a few minutes, he looked up, appearing a bit uneasy.

"I did find something. It seems there was an incident involving Ahana. She was taken in for questioning on suspicion of drug possession. We didn't have enough evidence to hold her, so she was released the same night," the officer said cautiously.

My heart sank, knowing that Ahana had been detained even if it was for a short period. "Do you have any idea where she might be now? Is there any other information you can provide?"

The officer hesitated for a moment before responding, "I'm sorry, but I can't disclose any further details. Our investigation didn't yield anything substantial, and we closed the case. If you want more information, you'll have to go through official channels."

I thanked the officer for his help. At least I had uncovered something about Ahana's arrest. As I left the police station, I realized that this was just the beginning of a deeper investigation, one that would require perseverance and determination to uncover the truth.

As I stood outside the police station, contemplating my next move, a lady constable approached me. She looked slightly hesitant but determined to share something important.

"Excuse me, sir," she said, "I overheard your conversation inside. I was there when Ahana was arrested, and I couldn't help but notice that the officer didn't give you the full story."

My curiosity piqued, and I urged her to continue. "Please, tell me everything you know. I need to find Ahana."

The constable took a deep breath before revealing the most important detail, "Ahana was indeed brought in on suspicion of drug possession, but she wasn't released that night. The truth is, she was taken away by a man named Digvijay."

"Digvijay? How can you be so sure?" I got intrigued.

"Because he personally came to take Ahana with him." The lady constable answered.

Chapter 30
(Parveen)

I felt a deep sense of despair as I walked towards the cell where Randhir was locked up in the police station. Mahesh was accompanying me. As we drew nearer, I saw the sad state Randhir was in. He lay still on the floor in the dimly lit cell, his body battered and bruised from the beating he had endured at the hands of the police. My heart sank at the sight, a lump forming in my throat.

Randhir slowly opened his eyes to look at us. He stared at Mahesh with contempt, his eyes blazing, and I could sense the rage that threatened to burst forth.

"Why is he here?" Randhir asked fuming in rage.

"He is trying to help..." I tried to reason but before I could say anything further, Randhir interrupted.

"Help? Do you know what this bastard did? He helped Ahana run away from home. He knew about her whereabouts all this time. He was the one who was feeding her with hatred for us. The police told me that. He even had the audacity to come to the police and tell them everything but did not have the guts to tell us, the parents who were wondering whether our child was even alive." Randhir's anger soon vanished, and his emotions got the better of him. He started to cry and fell on his knees. I, too, sat on my knees and held Randhir's face in my hands, trying to console him.

"I know everything, but believe me. He is trying really hard to help us now. You need to trust him," I tried to reason with Randhir, explaining that Mahesh was trying to help us find Ahana. I pleaded with my husband to let go of the bitterness and hatred, but he remained silent and unmoving. His injuries and the trauma of the situation had clearly taken a toll on him, and I feared he would never recover.

For a moment, the three of us stayed in an uncomfortable silence. I felt the weight of the situation pressing down on me like a heavy blanket, and I wished I could do something to ease the pain and anguish that Randhir was feeling. But all I could do was stand there and offer my support.

Finally, Mahesh spoke up, "I think I should go now," he said softly, his gaze shifting from Randhir to me. "I will do what I can to find Ahana."

I nodded. Maybe that was the only right thing to do at that moment. I started stroking Randhir's forehead gently as I tried to comfort him. I prayed that Ahana would be found and returned to us safely.

As I tried to console Randhir, my phone buzzed with a call from an unknown number. I glanced at the screen but chose to disconnect the call, wanting to focus on the situation at hand.

Randhir's was filled with confusion and frustration. "Why have the police arrested me now when the case of her murder was closed long back, and they had ruled it was a suicide? I just can't understand why I am being accused all over again."

I tried to stay calm and then told him about the video. "The police have actually received a video, a video of Ahana."

"What?" Randhir was confused.

"Yes, they say some unknown sources have sent them a video of Ahana where she claims to have seen you pushing your ex-wife from the roof of your house," I explained in the most rational way possible.

"But how...what are you talking about? How can this be possible?" Randhir was so full of confusion that it was difficult for him to even articulate his thoughts.

As the weight of this information sank in, Randhir experienced a mix of emotions. On one hand, he was relieved and overjoyed to know that Ahana was alive somewhere in this world. But on the other hand, he was deeply saddened to learn that she still believed he was responsible for her mother's death.

The unknown calls on my mobile persisted, and it began to worry me. 'Who could be calling repeatedly from an unknown number at such a crucial time?' I decided to ignore my phone for the moment so that I could fully focus on supporting Randhir through this distressing situation.

As we continued talking, Randhir expressed his desire to see the video that had led to his arrest. He hoped to understand why Ahana held such a belief and find a way to communicate with her. Perhaps there was a misunderstanding that needed to be cleared.

"We'll get the video. The lawyer is trying to get it, and he has also applied for your bail. You'll come out very soon. You need to be strong for my sake...Ahana's sake." I said, but I knew he was not listening. He was lost in his thoughts about the video and what could have led Ahana to say something like that.

My phone continued buzzing, and it was beginning to irritate me now.

"Who is calling you?" Randhir finally asked.

"I don't know. It's an unknown number."

"I think you should pick it up. It seems urgent."

I nodded and went a little far from the cell and picked up the call.

"Who is this?" I asked curtly.

"Where the fuck have you been? I have been calling you for so long. I need to see you. It's urgent." It was Ajay on the other end.

"I am sorry, but I can't come. I have sent my replacement for you. My husband and my family need me at this time." I was annoyed. This was the time for me to spend with my family, not being a nurse and fulfilling my duty towards Ajay.

"I am not going to listen to any excuses. Just come here. I have news for you, and this can help you. It is about Ahana." The last sentence that he said was a whisper, and I knew at that moment that it was urgent.

***

Ajay was on his bed, curled up like a cat, his phone held up to his face. He was watching something on the screen, a movie or a video – it was hard to tell – but the eager gleam in his eyes and the look of intense concentration on his face were enough to tell that it was something he was enjoying.

He was so immersed in whatever he was watching that he hadn't noticed that I had entered the room. When he realized my presence, he threw his phone away and started blabbering in a high-pitched tone.

"Oh, where the heck have you been? I tried calling you so many times," he exclaimed, almost jumping up from his bed. He was wearing a pair of loose sweatpants and an oversized t-shirt, and his face was beaming with an excitement that was almost palpable.

"I was at the police station. My husband got arrested last night," I said, and I almost felt like crying.

Ajay's eyes widened with shock. "Your husband? But why?" he asked incredulously. I had never seen such genuine curiosity in him before, and for a moment, I wondered what had changed in Ajay over the past few days.

Fighting hard to hold back my tears, I answered his question, "The police claim that he murdered his ex-wife and that it was not a suicide. They say they have some video of Ahana where she confessed about being a witness to the crime."

Suddenly, the room was plunged into thick and eerie silence. Then, Ajay cackled maniacally, as if some cruel inner demon had taken control of his mind. If he hadn't been bedridden, he would have bounced around the walls like a drunken clown, howling with laughter. Fury coursed through my veins as I glared at him. This is why he forced me to come here? To mock me with his sick humour?

"What are you doing?! Have you gone mad?! Oh, forgive me, I should've known that to be true long ago! You're nothing but a spoiled brat who's grown too accustomed to your father's wealth! You wretched little insect!" My words pierced through the air like bullets, but Ajay didn't answer. Instead, he stood motionless in the silent aftermath, looking completely traumatized by my outburst.

I said nothing for a while, and then suddenly, Ajay responded, "That's the real you. Now I can see you. I love this side of people where they start blurting out what's in their minds without using the filter of emotions. Emotions make us weak. We should speak our hearts out. You know that is the main reason why I love your daughter, Ahana."

The mention of Ahana made me rethink what and why I was there. Did he need to show me anything else from the dark web now? My stomach roiled with dread. What kind of terror had Ahana stumbled upon? My mind was filled with horrific and sinister possibilities; these thoughts wreaked havoc on my vulnerable heart. All I could do was stand there, unable to move or speak, feeling the panic slowly consuming me.

"What happened to Ahana now?" My voice had no emotion in it. I wanted answers, and my gaze was fixed on Ajay.

"Nothing," he said nonchalantly.

"Then why the heck did you call me here?" I shouted again, but this time with tears rolling down my eyes.

"To tell you that you can save your husband. He is innocent, but only if you will tell me the truth." For the first time, I sensed some emotions in Ajay's voice.

"How can you save him when you don't even know what happened to him?" I was confused. If he knew he could save him, that meant he knew what had happened to him; then why ask in the first place and laugh about it?

"I knew he was in jail, but I had no idea about the charges. This makes the whole thing so simple, and I really applaud the minds of those people who are playing against your family because they made it look like...like...what is the word? Forget the word. You got my feelings, right?" Ajay wanted me to respond to this, but it made no sense to me at all. I was still trying to make sense of what had unfolded with my gaze fixed on Ajay's eyes, which brimmed with curiosity and confusion.

"The summary of whatever I said or did is simple. If you are ready to tell me the truth, I am ready to save your family and your daughter as well," he spoke before leaning against his pillow and resting his back on the wall.

"What truth?" I asked.

"The truth about my father. I know that you know what I am talking about."

I was transfixed by the look in his eyes; they burned with an unspoken intensity that spoke volumes, revealing far more than words ever could. His gaze filled me with dread, leaving no doubt of the hidden message he was trying to convey.

Chapter 31
(Digvijay)

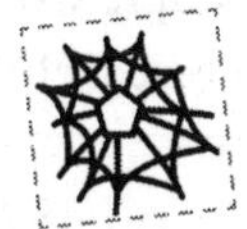

The young hacker shook his head incredulously, eyes wide with disbelief. "Sir, this is almost impossible," he murmured in a trembling voice. "That's why we use the dark web, to hide ourselves." His hands were shaking as if he was trying to ward off an unknown threat coming towards him, and my request for information about the sender of the email seemed to terrify him.

My voice thundered across the room with crushing force, sheer anger reverberating off the walls. "I don't give a damn! I want and need to know who this is, or else you're all fired! Got it?!" I unleashed my wrath upon my technical team, who were there to make money for me on the dark web, and these were the people who handled everything concerned with our show on Ahana.

I stormed out of the room, my heart pounding in my chest. Out of the corner of my eye, I could see Daisy swaggering seductively down the corridor towards me. She was wearing my favourite black skirt and red top, with her hair falling freely over her shoulders and those irresistible glasses perched upon her nose. Normally, I would have at least smiled on seeing her, but I was too consumed by fury to appreciate the sight. The email I had received only a few hours earlier echoed through my mind like an alarm bell—how did they know about me? About Ahana?

Randhir's public apology and confession and his subsequent arrest made it clear that something was wrong, and if the news continued to spread this way, people would soon believe that I was the mastermind behind it all. This could prove disastrous for my business. I had so many plans to execute, but if my image got hampered in the public eye, people would refrain from associating their name with me. I had to be careful, but before that, I wanted my revenge as well.

"Sir, I think we should get rid of Ahana now. Let us give her to Parag and get away from this whole mess," Daisy implored.

"No, not yet. I want to know who is trying to mess with me. I want them to understand that they cannot trifle with someone who holds power over everything."

I waited for a long time, contemplating how to respond to this mysterious person. Eventually, I wrote back:

What do you want exactly?

He replied promptly:

I want to meet Ahana once, all alone.

An admirer? Or a threat? Should I be worried about him? I had no choice but to take the risk and find out. He knew my name, so he clearly knew something about me.

I continued to stare at the email. I wanted to throw the laptop away, but curiosity and concern drove me to continue the conversation.

Why do you want to meet her alone?

His reply was short and cryptic:

That's none of your concern. I will tell you the time and place; you just need to bring her there.

Fury surged through me at his demand. How dare he threaten and command me? If he knew my name, didn't he understand how powerful I was? I seethed in anger as I imagined him ordering me around like a dog. Who does he think he is? His audacity was too much for me to bear.

I decided to take a different approach.

I won't bring her to you. If you want to meet her, you need to come to me.

The reply came almost immediately, and it was filled with menace.

You don't get to decide. If you don't follow my instructions, you'll regret it.

Oh yeah! Do you think you can order me, and I'll behave like a puppy? You love Ahana, right? Do you know what I can do to her? Do you want to see it? I am warning you anything that will happen to Ahana now will be your responsibility.

My fingers trembled as I furiously pressed the enter key, sending the scathing email. My jaw tightened, and my anger reached a boiling point, consuming me with its intensity. The taste of bile rose in my throat as I watched the message show up in my sent tab.

The unexpected reply didn't come almost immediately like all the other messages but took time. It said.

Oh yeah! Do you think you still own the world and everything circles around you? You love your business, right? Do you know what I can do about it? Do you want to see it? I am warning you, anything that will happen to your business now will be your...

Whoever was behind these messages deliberately left the three dots at the end. I knew it because all I did after reading the message was stare at those last three dots.

Within half an hour, many things changed.

Daisy burst through the door and threw down her files. Her phone was buzzing with notifications, and her voice quivered as she shouted urgently, "The stock prices are tanking! One of our investors got a tip about something shady in our books and just bailed. We've lost five per cent of our value in the last ten minutes alone! People are calling, demanding answers!"

My eyes darted to my ringing phone. Jhunjhunwala's name lit up the screen, and I knew I had to take the call. I picked up the phone, and before I could say a word, he began, "I had big plans with you, but I never deal with people who can't handle their own partners. I still have hopes for you. Do not let me down."

I thought that was it. But there was more to come.

Chapter 32
(Parveen)

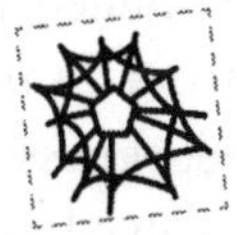

"If you are ready to tell me the truth, I am ready to save your family and your daughter as well."

"What truth?"

"The truth about my father. I know that you know what I am talking about."

My mouth opened to form some useless protestation, but I froze with the stark realization of what I had done. I had been poisoning this kid for ages now, and if his father was guilty, then I was too. Trembling like a leaf in a hurricane, I struggled to get the words out while his fierce gaze bore into me.

"I...I don't know..." I tried to speak, but the words didn't come out.

"Oh please. I knew everything from the very beginning. You think I am a fool lying in this bed for years, not realizing what goes on in this house? The truth is that I knew every damn thing that was happening. I knew you were an accomplice in his crime. But I don't blame you. You had no other choice, but I wanted to hear the words from your own mouth. I wanted to hear the exact words that my father used when he convinced you to follow his orders and try to kill me."

Ajay spoke mechanically, his voice devoid of emotion, plodding through the conversation as if nothing had any relevance to him at all.

"I never wanted to do it, but I had no other choice." I cried.

"I know. Didn't you hear me correctly? I knew it all."

The floor felt like quicksand, dragging me deeper into an unfamiliar realm. Panic threatened to overwhelm me until my phone vibrated with a call from Tanmay. At that moment, I was yanked out of the spiralling darkness, and back into reality where my problems remained unresolved and looming.

I anxiously picked up the call to hear what had happened in Delhi.

"Who is it?" Ajay immediately demanded, his voice tense and anxious.

"It's Tanmay," I said, my throat suddenly dry. "He is a friend, a journalist willing to help us find Ahana." I didn't know why I responded to Ajay's sharp enquiry; maybe to break away from our conversation and focus on locating Ahana.

"Keep the phone on speaker," Ajay said, and I did the same.

Tanmay gave us all the information he had been able to gather in Delhi so far, "I went to the college and got to know that she was last seen at a party at a pub where she got arrested by the police on the charges of consuming drugs or something. When I inquired about this at the police station, I got to know that Digvijay got a hold of Ahana, and since then, she has been missing."

The air was tense with the silence that hung in the room. I glanced at Ajay, whose expression was still as unreadable as stone. Then Tanmay's voice came through the speaker, "I had a hunch that Digvijay was the one who knew the whereabouts of Ahana, but I didn't know how to get under his skin."

In a sudden surge of excitement, Ajay snatched the phone and hissed in a strained growl, "How good are you as a journalist?"

Tanmay was taken aback by the male voice and the strange question. "Sorry?" he stammered.

"I mean, how long would it take to spread a particular piece of news across the country?" Ajay barked impatiently.

"Who are you?" Tanmay asked cautiously.

"Doesn't matter. Just answer me."

When Tanmay still didn't answer, I intervened.

"He is Ajay. Digvijay's son."

Tanmay took some time to make sense of what I had just said. He was not sure about talking in front of anyone related to Digvijay. I leaned over the phone and added, "He is here to help us. We can trust him."

As I said the words, Ajay smiled. For the first time, I saw him smiling in this way. It was a kind of smirk but a sweet one.

"I think I can do that pretty well. If the news is powerful, I have followers and resources to spread it within a couple of hours or maybe even less," Tanmay finally replied.

"Great. Have you heard about deep fake?" Ajay finally revealed what was on his mind.

Chapter 33
(Tanmay)

As soon as the cameraman signalled me with a thumbs up, I started my job.

"Good evening, viewers. I'm Tanmay, a freelance journalist, and tonight we begin with a gripping and mysterious update on the case of the missing girl, Ahana. As you may recall, she made headlines earlier for her allegations against Divya Hospital, which led to turmoil for its owner, renowned businessman Mr Digvijay Singh. Tonight, however, the spotlight is on a different twist in the case. Ahana's father has been arrested by the police on grave charges, shaking the foundation of this already perplexing case. But before we dive into the latest developments, I want to take you back to the journey that led me to Delhi."

A video edited by professionals to help people remember the events in a chronological manner was played about Ahana and her connection with the college in Delhi. The video ended, and my part began.

"I investigated further into the case and got to know that after the arrest, which by the way, is not registered in any of the official records of the police, Ahana just disappeared.

Ahana's disappearance has left the nation puzzled, but the recent turn of events has only intensified the intrigue. The police have apprehended her father, Randhir, on suspicion of murdering his ex-wife, Ahana's mother. It's a case that the police had previously ruled as a suicide, but a new video has emerged, changing the course of the investigation."

Ahana (in the video): (Emotional and fearful) I saw it all... that dreadful night. My father pushed my mother off the roof. It was not a suicide. He killed her!

"This video, sent by an anonymous sender, claims to feature Ahana as the witness to her mother's fatal fall. This crucial piece of evidence prompted the police to reopen the case and apprehend Randhir, as his daughter remains missing. The arrest raises numerous questions about the motive behind this shocking crime and Ahana's current whereabouts. But as usual, the police don't want to comment on anything. Even the video of Ahana that you just saw was not sent by the police to us, but we worked really hard to get it for our viewers. You can clearly see how afraid she appears. And now, before we conclude tonight's broadcast, we have one more video to share with you. Please be warned; the following content may be disturbing for some viewers."

My heart thumped as the video finally began to play, a maniacal sensation of fear and anticipation coursing through me. I felt like I was taking a leap into the unknown, and deep in my core, I knew this was wrong; as a journalist, I had no place meddling in this. But to save a life, I had to. This time, it wasn't just about the facts; it was much bigger than that.

Ahana: (Emotional and trembling) I... I don't know if anyone will believe me, but I need to share the truth. It's haunting me, eating me from the inside, and I can't bear the weight of this secret any longer. (Pauses, takes a deep breath) That fateful night, when everything changed, I was there, hidden in the shadows, a silent witness to a tragedy that shattered my world. I saw everything that night. It was...it was King Khan who pushed my mother off the roof. Just the same way he did in the movie Baazigar. I want justice for my mother.

"Doesn't the last video sound like fiction? Because it is fiction! Why would Shah Rukh Khan kill Ahana's mother? Huh! Bullshit! But it did look real, right? Ahana sounded convincing enough. But did she say it? Of course not. The video that you saw earlier and this one as well are the results of technology that the world fears. It is called a deep fake. Deep fake technology has raised significant concerns as it can be used maliciously to spread misinformation, defame individuals, or frame innocent people for crimes they did not commit. The case of Ahana's father, Randhir, being arrested based on a video featuring her, a missing person, sent by an unknown source is indeed alarming. It raises questions about the reliability of digital evidence in criminal investigations."

I took a pause and looked deep into the camera, realizing the weight of the words I was about to say. "Don't you think that this family has already suffered a lot? Randhir and Parveen have both tried very hard to bring their daughter back and are continuously fighting this battle with unknown powers who are trying to hide Ahana for some reason that is still unknown to us. Maybe one day, when Ahana reappears, the truth will come out as well. Till then, we can only wait to see if the police will still try to hide the main culprit or keep harassing the family fighting for their rights. I am Tanmay, and this is my fight against the powerful people hiding behind the masks of humanity."

The video spread rapidly, appearing on mobile devices, tablets, and television screens. As intended, the name Digvijay was connected to the case, leading the police to drop their case against Randhir due to lack of evidence. The plan had worked, but there was still work to be done. The real problem was still upon us. We needed to find Ahana and find her soon because now, Digvijay would not wait before taking even harsher steps.

Chapter 34
(Digvijay)

I was angry, sitting in my office. Everything I had gained through this game of power and exploitation was slipping away from me, and the media and public opinion were ready to declare me a criminal. I sat silent, my phone buzzing constantly. Daisy, my secretary, stood at my side, saying nothing. My eyes were fixed on the television where a news channel was playing the video of Ahana on a loop.

My face contorted in rage as I watched, and an unstoppable force of anger bubbled up in my chest. With a violent thrust, I punched the screen of my TV, shattering it beyond repair. Shards of glass scattered across the floor, and the room fell silent.

Daisy gasped, her hands coming to her mouth to stifle a scream as she was scared of seeing my violent reaction. My shoulders slumped, and I let out a deep breath. I had been trying to save my sinking boat, but nothing was going in my favour.

I felt as though I was losing control, and it brought a feeling of helplessness with it. Everything I had worked so hard for was crumbling around me, and I felt powerless to do anything to stop it.

I looked over at Daisy, who was still standing in shock. When she saw me looking at her, she broke her silence. "What are you going to do?" she asked.

I let out a deep and heavy sigh, running a hand through my hair and shaking my head. "I don't know," I said, my voice filled with resignation.

I knew I had to do something, but I couldn't think of what that could be. The media worked like a well-oiled machine, and it seemed like no matter what I did, I wouldn't be able to stop it from running.

I slumped back in my chair and looked out the window, watching the sunlight streaming in. I needed a plan, and I needed it fast.

Closing my eyes, I tried to think, but I was so overwhelmed by the situation that I couldn't focus. I felt like I was standing at the edge of a cliff and about to fall.

"Sir, I have another piece of news for you. The politician Parag is trying extremely hard to contact us. Our servers are detecting attacks from various unknown sources, and when we tried to get the information about it, one name that came out was Parag. He has hired a bunch of technicians to crack our servers, but he doesn't know that these technicians basically work for us."

Suddenly, it came to me. A plan that could work. I opened my eyes and turned to Daisy.

"Bring me my laptop," I said to Daisy, and she rushed out of the room without asking any other questions and obliged.

I logged into my laptop and began typing the response to the mail that I received from the unknown user.

When and where?

I typed just three words in the response to the previous mail.

You'll leave her in a car parked at 22nd Milestone Cafe on the highway tomorrow at 6 pm, and from there, we'll guide you further. As she doesn't know how to drive, you'll be the driver for her. No one else should follow.

The response came soon and excitement surged through me. How does this man know the personal details about Ahana? Who is this man? I was eager to find out.

Before I got lost in the excitement for tomorrow, I had to do one more thing. I wrote one more email.

Tomorrow at 6 pm in the parking lot of 22nd Milestone Cafe on the highway.

I wrote and sent the mail.

Daisy looked at me with concern in her eyes, her worry evident. "Are you sure this plan will work?" she asked cautiously.

I looked back at her, my determination unwavering. "If this doesn't work, nothing will work," I replied firmly. "I need to find out who's behind all of this, who's trying to ruin me. And I won't rest until I do."

Daisy nodded, understanding my resolve, but she couldn't hide her apprehension. "But will this plan save our business?" she asked, voicing her concern.

"I don't care about the business now. I just want my revenge. I want to see who the fuck is trying to mess with me."

Chapter 35 (Ahana)

My eyes slowly fluttered open as I found myself in a dream world. It was a familiar realm, a place I often escaped to in the corners of my mind. In this dream, I was walking through a serene park with my best friend, Jasmeen. The setting sun painted the sky in hues of orange and pink, casting a warm glow over the world around us.

Jasmeen smiled warmly at me, her eyes filled with understanding and compassion. "You know, Ahana, I feel safe around you."

I smiled back weakly, "I don't know, Jasmeen. I think it's the other way around. It feels like everything is falling apart. I can't seem to control anything. It's like I'm trapped in a maze of darkness. Is there an end to our suffering in this place?"

Jasmeen gently placed a hand on my shoulder, giving me a reassuring squeeze. "I know it's not easy, but remember, I'm here for you. You don't have to face these demons alone. Together, we can conquer them. You are not defined by your struggles but by how you rise above them."

The comforting words began to penetrate my troubled mind, giving me a glimmer of hope. We continued moving ahead, holding hands and swaying as if we cared about nothing in this world. Then we reached a bench, where we sat down, still facing the setting sun. Jasmeen continued, "My existence depends on your trust in me. Trust is the only thing that is keeping me alive. If this trust ever falters, I won't be able to save you. Remember that."

"Jasmeen!" Someone shouted from a distance. I looked everywhere but found no one around. My heart raced as I found myself all alone in the park.

Then came another shout, "Ahana!"

I then felt a push, hard enough to make me fall on the ground, but there was no ground beneath me. I kept falling. I shouted, and then my eyes opened in shock. I was on a bed, the same bed. And there, standing by my bed, was the face that haunted my nightmares – Digvijay.

"Ahana," Digvijay sneered, a sinister grin spreading across his face. "Where's your friend Jasmeen? Call her. We are going for a long drive."

***

Digvijay remained silent as we drove on. He was not interested in me, he always liked Jasmeen more. After what felt like an eternity, I felt the fresh air of the outside world. There was some strange happiness in me that wanted to burst forth but I kept it hidden. I didn't want to give any wrong ideas to Digvijay.

In my exhaustion and anxiety, my eyelids grew heavy, and I could no longer fight the sleep that beckoned me. My body slumped against the car seat, and I drifted into a restless slumber.

As I slept, something extraordinary was happening. Within the depths of my subconscious mind, Jasmeen emerged, taking control of my body. Her presence was powerful, even the chauffeur who was driving the car silently noticed the sudden change that happened within me through the rear-view mirror.

"At least you could have asked formally before taking me to dinner. I would have dressed more sophisticatedly for you," Jasmeen said.

Digvijay turned and smiled, "Finally you are here. You took time this time."

"So, who's the client tonight?" Jasmeen asked.

"This one is special. A lot of memories will surface. You'll have a great time." Digvijay commented. He smiled but his words were full of anger.

* * *

Finally, we arrived at our destination. Jasmeen caught sight of a sign which said 22nd Milestone Cafe from the corner of her eye as we pulled into the parking lot. Before we had a chance to exit the car, Digvijay handcuffed me and gagged me with a cloth. Fear coursed through me, and I chose to keep my eyes shut, not wanting to witness what might happen next. Jasmeen was there to take care of me. I knew she'd handle everything without fear.

Digvijay stepped out of the car and moved towards another vehicle parked nearby, leaving me with a sense of unease. I noticed that our chauffeur wasn't following us, indicating that Digvijay intended to drive himself. He moved to the car, opened the door, and forcefully made me sit in the backseat before taking the driver's seat. The world outside felt like a blur, and I could only rely on Jasmeen's presence to keep me grounded.

A buzzing noise emanated from somewhere inside the car, and Digvijay searched for the source. After finding the phone in the cabinet next to him, he answered the call and began driving, possibly receiving instructions on his phone to guide him about the route.

The uncertainty of our destination and Digvijay's intentions weighed heavily on my mind, but I remained resolute, knowing that Jasmeen was doing everything she could to protect and help me. Despite the darkness surrounding us, I held on to a glimmer of hope that we would find a way to escape this nightmare.

***

I was curled up in a ball, my face pressed against the backseat, with my wrists handcuffed behind me. Digvijay was driving the car, his steely eyes barely glancing in the rear-view mirror at me. We were headed to an unknown place, and all I could see out of the windows was a blur of trees and darkness.

I squirmed in the cramped back seat of the car as he drove dangerously on this unfamiliar road with no apparent destination. The darkness outside filled me with dread and despair as I looked out. I had no idea where he was taking me and why he had handcuffed me. Jasmeen told me that maybe he did all this because he was afraid that I would run away.

The car screeched to a stop, and he jumped out. For a few seconds, I heard nothing, and I thought he had left me behind in some deserted place, but then I heard his laughter. His laughter echoed in the night, its haunting cadence sending chills up my spine. The darkness seemed to swallow him whole as his voice gradually faded away.

"So here you all are! A little family reunion, huh? And Mahesh as well? When did you start talking with Randhir? When did you guys catch up?" The mention of Mahesh uncle and Randhir, my father, filled me with joy. I wanted to come out, but Jasmeen held me back. She said it was some kind of trap and I shouldn't fall for it. I wanted to open my eyes and come out, but Jasmeen held me. "I am here to help you. You stay back," she ordered. I followed her instructions and kept my eyes closed, but I could feel the comforting presence of my family around.

Was it the end of my suffering? I wanted to run away from the car and hug my family, but I couldn't move.

"You little bastard." The laughter that once filled the air suddenly died, replaced by Digvijay's stern and angry voice.

"Surprised?" I heard someone else but couldn't recognize that voice.

"You think I am surprised? Really? You are still a child, my son. Just look around you. Do you think you set a trap for me, and I ended up here against my will because of your perfect planning? You all are fools then. From the day you began messing with my business, I knew it was you. Who else could have gotten his hands on the secret files of my office? It could only be you. But the thing that made me wonder was why you are so obsessed with Ahana, but then I figured out the reason for it as well. I just had to link Parveen and Ahana, and ta-da, I understood your hidden agenda. And one more thing, I had some doubts at the back of my mind whether it was someone else but you confirmed this with your choice of location—the 22nd Milestone Cafe. You fucker, isn't this the place where we used to come to grab quick ice cream when we stayed here, in this apartment?"

"What is he talking about? You used to live here?" It was a familiar voice, my father's voice.

Panic coursed through me, and I thrashed wildly in the backseat, like a wild animal caged for slaughter. The rough material jammed into my mouth muffled my screams, but I still tried to scream until my throat was raw. A glimmer of hope flickered as I heard footsteps approaching, but it was quickly extinguished when the car door opened and I saw Digvijay.

He dragged me out of the car, and that's when I saw everyone. My eyes fell on a scene that I could have never imagined. My father, my uncle, and Parveen, all three were standing together. There was one more person whom I didn't recognize, a child in a wheelchair. He didn't look well. Why was he here? And who was he? Jasmeen was on red alert. She shut me up once again and took charge of my body.

"Jasmeen or Ahana? Who am I talking to?" Digvijay asked.

"Who do you think?" Jasmeen replied and eyed Digvijay. She never lost her confidence.

"Awesome. Then you must be wondering what exactly is happening here, right?" Digvijay smiled.

"If you wish to tell, I am all ears," Jasmeen replied.

"That child, that fluffy child in the wheelchair is my son. He just betrayed me to get hold of you. Apparently, he is a very big fan of you and had placed many bets on you while you were locked with Ahana in my dungeon. He was one of the sadists because of whom your Ahana had to suffer every day." Digvijay introduced Jasmeen to his son, and the description he gave made me angry. It was enough for me to boil up in anger. Jasmeen noticed the sudden change in me. She eyed the child, but the child gave no response. Digvijay continued, "Next to him is the person who killed your mother, Ahana's father, Randhir, and married the other woman, Parveen, the woman who is standing next to him. And lastly, your favourite uncle Mahesh, who was the first one to approach the police with your whereabouts in Delhi and helped them to arrest you and take you back to me." Digvijay took a long pause and then concluded, "What a lovely reunion."

Mahesh uncle suddenly got defensive and blurted out, "No, Jasmeen, you know me. I haven't done anything wrong. You do know how much I love you. This man is fooling you with his lies."

Digvijay started to laugh. "Yes, yes, he does love you a lot. He loves small kids a lot. He is famous in the whole town for his 'activities' with children."

Digvijay's words sent Mahesh uncle in a terrifying rage causing his knuckles to turn white as he clenched his fists. He was enraged, but he stayed rooted to the spot, not moving a muscle.

As everyone fell quiet, assessing the situation in their own ways, Digvijay spoke again, "So tell me, what's the plan now?

I don't have all the time in the world. Have you informed the police? Are they coming? Because I need to prepare for that as well."

My father suddenly came running towards me, to which Digvijay responded quickly, "Nah, nah, stay back. She is still my patient. She's still in my control. And if you don't obey, I have other means as well."

He whipped out the gun from his jacket, causing everyone present to step back. Fear reverberated through the air as Digvijay's cold and calculated movements became crystal clear.

Then Digvijay asked his question again, "Now tell me, how will we proceed? What was your plan, my boy?"

He fixed his gaze on his son, whose motionless body was confined to a wheelchair. The weight of the entire situation seemed to press down on him at that moment as if the world around them had transformed into an oppressive force. His son sat silently, not daring to move, seemingly aware of the gravity of the moment.

"Well, frankly speaking, this is the first time I have come out of my house, and I can tell you one thing for sure, I am loving the whole scene right now. It is looking like we are living the climax scene of some '90s Bollywood movie where the villain has everything under control, and soon the police will come in and take all of us under arrest." The son finally spoke, and these were definitely not the words that anyone was expecting. Jasmeen suddenly smiled; no one else responded.

"Can someone please remove that cloth from her mouth? It's hurting her." Suddenly, Parveen interjected. She saw the blood oozing out from the corner of my mouth.

Digvijay said nothing and simply removed the cloth. Jasmeen was still smiling, and finally, she addressed Digvijay, "This kid is yours? I doubt it because he's got a good sense of humour, unlike you."

The kid and Jasmeen both looked at each other and smiled and then Jasmeen said, "But that doesn't mean we can be friends. Actually, the thing is, I don't want to see any of your faces here." She suddenly changed her demeanour.

"And you, stop pretending that you care, alright?" Jasmeen went for Parveen this time and barked at her. My father sensed Jasmeen's presence in me and got in between, "You can't talk to her like that. You are not our daughter. You are just an imposter living in her. You are creating hell for my daughter. The reason for her suffering is none other than you, Jasmeen. I haven't said a word to you because I thought you were trying to help Ahana, but I was wrong. I should have countered you earlier.

"Mahesh, are you listening? This is the reason why I wanted to keep her away from you. Jasmeen wanted to talk to you and not my little angel. She was not the kind of girl who would venture out looking for love before talking to her own family. She knew and still knows that her father loved her. I never thought..." His words hung in the air as Jasmeen interjected, her voice cutting through the tension like a scythe, "Oh, shut up! you murderer," Jasmeen finally said, crossing the line.

"Am I the murderer? Am I, Jasmeen?" Suddenly Jasmeen stopped abruptly. I wanted to wake up. I wanted Jasmeen to go away for a moment and let me talk to my father, and sort things out, but Jasmeen was not listening.

"Shut your mouth and stay put! I am in complete control of this situation. Let me handle it,' Jasmeen snarled at me, her anger palpable in the air as I tried to resist. 'I want to talk. He's my father; you cannot say these things to him! Remember our agreement?!" My voice quaked as I spoke, but she seemed to be deaf to my request.

"Hey, hey, hey! Stop. I am not here to listen to all your family drama. Is there anyone who will call the police or not?" Digvijay roared.

"What will the police do? We all know that they are working under your command," Randhir's voice dropped to a dejected whisper.

"Why are you so eager to have the police around?" Mahesh asked Digvijay.

"Well, so that I can start taking my revenge. I have at least two people here to kill and a great story to cover my tracks. Want to hear?" No one said anything. Digvijay then asked Jasmeen, "I am sure you'll love to hear the story. Listen, the media is my biggest enemy at the moment, that we all can agree, right? What can turn the tide for me on the media front? A sympathy story. So, here's the story. Randhir thinks that I took his daughter away from him. So, he called me to this deserted place with my son and killed him in front of my eyes." Digvijay looked deep into his son's eyes while he took a long pause, "Then, I had a scuffle with Randhir and got his gun and killed him in self-defence, of course."

"No, you can't do that. We won't let you do it," Parveen said, the fear of what Digvijay was capable of clearly visible on her face.

"Can you stop me? Can you? If you had the guts to stop me, why didn't you try stopping me when I hired you to kill my son? Does your husband know about it? And Ahana? Anyone?" Parveen averted her gaze from everyone. It was evident by her expressions that there was definitely something that she was hiding. Digvijay continued, "Well, I just changed my mind. I can't leave witnesses, right? I need to kill two more people then." Mahesh and Parveen both knew who he was talking about.

"And what about me, then?" Jasmeen asked.

"You, my darling, you are my precious. I'll take you back to my place," Digvijay smiled. I felt the fear rising in my veins. I didn't want to go back.

"Just stay put. Nothing will happen to you," Jasmeen told me, but I was not feeling the comfort in her words. I was shaking with fear. "He'll kill us all. He'll kill us all." I started crying. "Oh, shut up. You need to grow up, Ahana."

The son, who was sitting and listening in silence, suddenly burst out laughing. "You know what, Dad? You are very predictable when it comes to your planning. I knew it was only a matter of time until you pulled something like this. And that is why, just for your information, I've got my team ready to expose your 'ventures' on the dark web, and by tomorrow morning, it will be all over the news. So, that means that Ahana is definitely not going back there, and even if you kill us all here, you won't be going back to your comfortable life either."

Everyone fell silent and then suddenly Digvijay let out a cackle that reverberated across the emptiness. "All of you are so predictable!" He sneered with contempt. With an evil glint in his eyes, he declared, "Well, it's time I show you how I can turn things around. Prepare yourselves for a surprise!"

Digvijay pulled his mobile out of his pocket and called someone, saying, "You can come now."

Everyone waited to see what Digvijay had up his sleeve. Moments later, the door opened, and a man walked onto the scene with slow, unsure steps.

"Meet my backup plan," Digvijay said with a wicked grin. "The famous politician of our country, Mr Parag."

Chapter 36

Parag had been driving for what felt like endless hours, and finally, he reached the location he had received on his mobile. His throat was parched from the dry air; at last, after so long, he was about to meet Ahana. He exhaled the breath he had been holding, relieved to have found his destination.

He had been specifically instructed to wait outside a building until he received a call, and that's exactly what he did. He couldn't afford to let the only chance to free Ahana go to waste. Informing the police was an option, but he couldn't risk Ahana's life. Finally, his phone buzzed, and he stepped inside the building.

Parag stopped in his tracks, utterly confused. The building was occupied by a handful of people, two of whom he recognized — Digvijay and Randhir, Ahana's father. He had no idea what these two were doing there, but then Parag's eyes fell on Ahana.

As he moved closer, Parag could see that Ahana's hands were bound together in handcuffs. Panic rushed through him; what was going on here?

He stepped forward, and soon his panic transformed into anger.

"What is going on here?" he asked, his voice shaking with intensity.

No one replied. He turned to Digvijay, who was standing next to Ahana, and demanded, "Who has the key to these handcuffs?"

Digvijay smiled and extended his hand for a shake. "Hello, Mr Parag. I am Digvijay, and I am the one in charge of the situation here. You are just a pawn in the game, so please behave like one. Alright?"

Parag's heart raced as he looked at Ahana, who seemed scared and helpless, her dark eyes filled with fear. He knew he had to do something.

He stepped forward and addressed Digvijay firmly, "Please, she is my friend. I have already done what you asked, so why all this? I am here to take her with me, so why are you behaving like this? I don't understand."

Nobody moved. Parag felt desperate. He wanted to help Ahana, to free her from this terrible situation and take her away from this hell.

He took a deep breath and stepped even closer until he was standing right in front of Ahana. He looked her straight in the eyes and said in a soft yet determined voice, "Ahana, it's me. Parag. Don't worry, nothing bad will happen to you. I'm here to help you."

Ahana stared at him, her eyes wide with confusion. She didn't seem to recognize him.

Parag's heart sank. He had hoped that his presence would bring her some comfort, that she would remember him from their childhood days. But it seemed that she had no recollection of him.

"She doesn't remember you," Jasmeen replied. Parag had no knowledge of Jasmeen; he had thought it was Ahana. Parag was shocked, but he reached out and gently placed his hand on Ahana's shoulder. "It's okay," he said. "I'm here now. I won't let anything bad happen to you. I promise."

Ahana continued to look at him, still confused.

"Alright, enough of the drama now. Let me begin with the final part of my plan," Digvijay said with a smirk, "as I introduce you to Parag. He is very fond of Ahana for reasons unknown to me—love, affection, friendship, or maybe lust. I don't care. I just know he was desperate to free Ahana. In his pursuit, he has done many things to taint his career, and now it is almost impossible for him to regain what he has lost. But the biggest blunder he made was recently hiring a team of hackers to get to me through the dark web, without knowing that the team was working for me. So, my son," Digvijay looked at Ajay and continued, "you won't be able to frame me for the dark web thing because my team has already taken care of everything. When the police or CBI try to investigate, they will realize that it was not me but Parag who was behind everything."

There was silence for a while, and then Digvijay pulled out his gun once again and asked, "So tell me, who wants to die first?"

Ajay picked up his phone in the meantime.

"Whom are you calling, the police? Should I begin my drama, then? Randhir, will you be the one to die first?" Digvijay smiled; it was all just a fun game for him.

"No, Dad! I have a small surprise for you as well. Let her come."

Everyone waited and looked at the door. The unfolding scene was unimaginable. Digvijay's mouth dropped when he saw who walked in — it was Daisy, Digvijay's assistant.

As soon as Daisy stepped inside the room, Digvijay shouted at her in a demanding tone, "What are you doing here?" She remained silent, her gaze shifting apprehensively between Digvijay and Ajay.

It was Ajay's turn to speak, "Why don't you tell him your true identity and who brought you here?"

Daisy inhaled deeply before finally replying, "My name is Chhaya. I was recruited by Ajay sir."

"No! That cannot be correct. What are you saying?!" Digvijay spat out, confusion prominent in his voice.

Ajay then smiled cunningly and asked, "Do you remember the first day when you met her? She just walked in, and you assumed she would be your personal assistant."

Daisy, who was actually Chhaya, interjected with a hint of bitterness, "Actually, he didn't even look at my face. His eyes were finding it difficult to come above my chest area."

The atmosphere thickened with palpable tension as Digvijay felt the burning shame of his actions. His face twisted into a combination of embarrassment and anger.

Ajay's voice rose to a crescendo, his words hitting each person like blades of blazing fire, "So, here is the moral of the story: I knew all that you did about the plan. That's why it doesn't even exist anymore. It is gone!" He finished with an air of finality and victorious glee.

Digvijay's rage boiled over. He felt betrayed by Chhaya and furious with Ajay's deceit. He pointed his gun at Chhaya and yelled, "You little traitor! How dare you deceive me like this!"

Chhaya stood her ground, her eyes steely with determination. "I did what I had to do to survive. I was just doing my job," she replied defiantly.

"You will regret this!" Digvijay shouted, his hand trembling with anger as he held the gun.

Chhaya moved with lightning speed, her hands darting forward and grabbing the gun from Digvijay in one fluid motion. In an instant, she had flipped the gun around, pointing it back at Digvijay. Everyone was taken aback by her swiftness and poise. Her face was set and determined as she held Digvijay's gaze, her finger resting lightly on the trigger of the gun.

Ajay said, "Didn't I tell you before? She is trained in martial arts. You should have known this if you had bothered to read her resume." Ajay smiled and paused for a while. After a moment, he added, "Now, here's the change in plan. We have gathered all the evidence to prove you guilty of everything you did to Ahana and Parag. Parag will help us strengthen the case against you, so you won't be able to manipulate the system as you always have. Ahana will finally be free and reunited with her family."

Digvijay's face contorted with anger and desperation. "And what about you?" he asked Ajay. "You do know you won't live much longer, right? It's all because of that woman Parveen. She's the same woman who became the reason for your mother's death as well, Ahana. Are you truly willing to return to that house and face the consequences?"

"I don't understand anything. What are we talking about here? I came here to take Ahana with me. She is not going anywhere." Now it was the time for Parag to get stubborn.

As the tense situation escalated, Jasmeen's anger reached its peak. She couldn't bear the thought of Ahana leaving with anyone else, not even her own family.

"Ahana will go with them, Ahana will go with me...what is this? Ahana is not going anywhere. She will stay with me. She is not a toy; she is a real person with feelings that no one understands," Jasmeen shouted, her voice filled with desperation.

Randhir tried to approach Ahana, but Jasmeen was not willing to let him get close. She took a step back as if protecting Ahana from any harm.

"No. Ahana, you listen to me," Randhir pleaded.

"You know what I have done for you so far. You can't listen to this murderer," Jasmeen reasoned with Ahana.

"Stop calling me a murderer!" Randhir retorted fiercely. "You know, Jasmeen. You know everything."

Randhir's composure started to crumble, and he began to lose control of his emotions.

"I know you. You killed your wife to get this woman in our house," Jasmeen accused.

"It was not me, goddammit. It was you! You were the one who pushed her off the roof, Jasmeen," Randhir shouted back, his voice choked with sorrow and anger.

Ahana remained silent, torn between the two people she cared about deeply. Everyone in the room was stunned, their eyes fixed on Randhir, who had just made a shocking revelation.

The weight of the accusation hung heavily in the air. Tears streamed down Randhir's face as he confronted the truth he had been suppressing for so long. The realization of what he had done was overwhelming, and guilt consumed him.

Ahana felt a mix of emotions, torn between her love for her father and the shocking revelation of her mother's death. She had always believed her mother's death was an accident, but now the truth had been exposed.

Ahana's heart wrenched in pain as she witnessed her father's breakdown. She wanted to console him, but she also couldn't ignore the truth that had come to light.

Finally, unable to bear the weight of it all, Ahana spoke in a soft, trembling voice, "I need some time to process all of this. Please, no...it was...it was a suicide, right? She was suffering from some mental trauma after my birth and that is why she...it was not a murder. Jasmeen? No, no, you are all wrong."

"You do remember the night, Ahana. It's just that Jasmeen is not letting you see things clearly. For once, just for once, listen to me and not your Jasmeen and you'll see things very clearly." Randhir was crying but continued talking to Ahana. Parveen was also crying seeing the scene unfold. Mahesh was feeling guilty because he had always thought that it was Randhir who killed

Nandini to marry Parveen but now after listening to everything, he was finding it difficult to fathom.

Ahana was struggling with her emotions, torn between wanting to confront Jasmeen about her father's accusation and the need to understand the truth about her mother's death. Jasmeen, on the other hand, was trying to shield Ahana from any further distress until they could resolve the situation.

"We'll talk about it later. Do not get hyper. You know me, right?" Jasmeen tried to reassure Ahana, her voice tinged with concern.

"But I think I do remember..." Ahana tried to recall the night but Jasmeen stopped Ahana forcefully.

"You remember nothing. You just remember me and my ways to make you stay away from all the troubles of life. I have always tried to help you and that is the only truth of life. You won't be able to survive for even a day without me. Understood?" Jasmeen yelled.

As Jasmeen was controlling Ahana, in another part of the room, Digvijay was stealthily making his way towards the gun that was now in Chhaya's possession. He had lost control of the situation, and desperation fuelled his actions.

His heart pounded as he closed in on the gun, his mind racing with thoughts of revenge and escape. When he finally got close to the weapon, he pushed Chhaya with all his strength and took hold of the gun. A sinister grin crossed his face.

Without hesitation, Digvijay fired a shot at Chhaya, who had been recovering from the shock of a sudden blow. The bullet hit her stomach, and she cried out of pain. After struggling for a moment, she died on the spot.

Seeing his chance, Digvijay turned towards Randhir, intending to take revenge on a man who had been a constant obstacle in his life. However, before he could pull the trigger, Ahana leapt at him, trying to disarm him once more.

The struggle was intense, and in the chaos, another shot rang out. Ahana felt a searing pain in her side and stumbled back, her hand clutching the wound.

Time seemed to slow down as everyone in the room froze realizing what had just happened. Ahana looked down, her vision blurred with tears and saw the blood staining her clothes.

"Ahana!" Jasmeen cried out in horror and took control of Ahana with an intensity few had seen before, like a wild animal on the hunt. In a single moment of fury, she had taken complete control over her body and mercilessly sat over the chest of Digvijay and punched his face until he lay motionless beneath her. Jasmeen yanked the gun from his lifeless hands, her fingers trembling with rage as she repeatedly pressed the trigger until it ran out of bullets. The walls and the whole body of Ahana were sprayed red with blood as everyone scrambled to rescue her. With one last breath, Jasmeen's eyes shut for the final time, and her body slumped to the ground.

Chapter 37
EPILOGUE

AHANA

I woke up in a hospital room, my body aching and groggy from whatever sedative had kept me unconscious. I heard the beeping of monitors and sensed the faint smell of sterilized air. For a moment, I panicked at the unfamiliar surroundings, before slowly remembering what had happened.

On the chair next to me, I saw Parveen sleeping awkwardly, a deep crease etched between her eyebrows due to the uncomfortable position. She stirred when I moved, her eyes opening to find me looking at her.

"Ahana," she said, her voice soft and gentle, "How are you feeling now?"

I tried to take a deep breath, but the pain in my side made me gasp instead. "I'm okay," I said. "Where's my father?"

At that moment, my father walked in, carrying a small bag in one hand. He stopped abruptly when he saw me awake, and then he smiled, the wrinkles around his eyes crinkling with relief.

He put the bag down and came to hug me, his arms encircling me in a warm embrace. I melted into him for a moment, happy to feel his presence after so long, before I flinched slightly as the pain in my side reminded me of my injuries.

Father stepped back, a look of worry on his face. "I'm sorry," he said. "Did it hurt?"

"No," I said. "It's okay. This will heal soon."

There was an uneasy silence between us, and I knew that there was something he wasn't telling me. I looked at Parveen, who was standing quietly at the foot of the bed.

"How's Jasmeen?" I asked, my voice barely above a whisper. "Did she survive?"

Father and Parveen exchanged a look, and I knew the answer before either of them said a word. "She died, right?" I said. "She died saving me."

The tears started flowing, and I felt a huge lump in my throat as the pain of her loss hit me. I had known her since childhood, and she had been a loyal friend to me for years. Losing her felt like a physical blow, and the pain of it was almost unbearable.

PARVEEN

My heart raced when Ahana spoke of Jasmeen. Could it be true? Was fate giving us a second chance? I dared to glance at Randhir only to find that we shared the same glimmer of hope in our eyes. My mind flooded with memories of all the moments when I had really tried to connect with Ahana and make this feel like a family, even though she had grown distant. In that moment I felt a surge of determination wash over me — this was what I had been fighting for and I would do anything to keep my family together.

A few days later, when Ahana came back and started living with us, I saw a change in her behaviour. She was more loving towards her father and me as well. She wanted to ensure that everyone around her was happy.

One day after the dinner was over, I was busy cleaning the utensils when Ahana came and stood next to me.

"Do you need anything, Ahana?" I asked her, puzzled.

"I just... I wanted to say sorry for everything. I never treated you well. I..." She wanted to say more, but I cut her short.

"It was not all your fault Ahana. I am responsible as well," I lowered my gaze.

"Can we start everything all over again?" Ahana said and smiled.

Later, on that same night, when I went to the bedroom, Randhir was on the bed, waiting for me to come. As soon as I sat next to him, I saw him in tears. Before I could ask anything, he said, "I have never seen Ahana so happy. It is all because of you. I just can't thank you enough." Randhir hugged me like a child and started to cry. I looked up and thanked my stars for everything. Finally, I had the family. I had always wished for.

RANDHIR

My feet carried me down the long hallway of the hospital. I was a free man, and for the first time in my life, I was able to walk unencumbered. I inhaled deeply, realizing that now things were in my favour after a long time.

The sun shone brightly in the sky, and the world around me burst with life and promise. I had been wrongfully accused of killing my beloved wife, and some also accused me of kidnapping my own daughter. But now, I felt a wave of relief wash over me.

As I entered the room, I saw my daughter sitting on the bed. She was awake. I almost ran towards her, and I hugged her tightly, grateful for the love and warmth she brought me. I had missed her terribly during my difficult days, and I had never been so relieved to see her beautiful face.

We held each other in silence for a few moments, my heart filled with joy, and the reality of my freedom finally sinking in. When we finally broke apart, I looked into her eyes and smiled.

She then asked about Jasmeen. We had nothing to tell her, but I was glad she had her own answer ready. She believed that

Jasmeen had died on that fateful night. I hoped that this would be the end of Jasmeen for her.

"I'm so glad to have you back," I said, my voice full of emotion.

She nodded, smiling back at me as tears ran down her cheeks.

"Come on," I said, "let's go home."

AJAY

Parveen had been pushing me relentlessly to visit a doctor for the last few months, but I had been stubbornly refusing her. I was insistent that nothing could save me now. I just wanted to spend the rest of my life living it on my own terms.

But, as much as I kept telling myself that, I had been feeling more and more exhausted and fatigued, almost like I was running on fumes. My body kept aching, and I was having difficulty sleeping, staying active, and focusing on the tasks at hand throughout the day. Seeing my struggle, Parveen offered to come with me to a doctor. After months of constant pushing and nagging, I had finally decided to go.

We went to the doctor, and after introducing me, Parveen started to tell him about my medical history.

The doctor then asked me some questions about my lifestyle and habits. He enquired about how much sleep I was getting, what kind of food I was eating, how much time I was spending outdoors, and my overall activity levels. After listening to my responses, he examined me thoroughly.

When the doctor was done with the examination, he said one thing to me, "If you cooperate with me and follow my instructions, I can help you feel better." He even suggested some lifestyle changes and prescribed some medicines. He also advised me to get some tests done just to be sure.

When I got home, I took the doctor's words seriously and started to make the suggested changes in my lifestyle. I spent more time outdoors, ate healthier, and took better care of myself. I also made sure to stick to the prescriptions and went for the tests that the doctor had advised me to get. I wanted the change. I thought if Ahana could do it, I could do it as well. There were times when Ahana, too, came to meet me. We sat and talked about various things but never about those dark days. I had found a friend in her. Maybe she found one in me as well.

TANMAY

With the help of Ajay, I set out on a mission to get justice for the wrongdoings of Digvijay. I was determined to bring down the corrupt hospital owner and his businesses. It had been weeks since I began my search for evidence and leads, and I had been gathering information from all possible sources. Ajay's assistance proved invaluable every step of the way.

I linked Digvijay's misdeeds with the dark web, sparking a national debate on such illicit activities. The evidence I had collected was enough to prove that the hospital was engaged in unethical practices. However, to make a solid case against Digvijay himself, I needed to establish his direct involvement. Months of searching led me to a crucial document with his unmistakable signature on it. This was the piece of evidence I needed to secure a conviction.

Presenting our evidence to the police and the media, we garnered significant coverage and public support. People rallied behind us, demanding justice for the patients who had been exploited by the hospital and Digvijay. Finally, the hospital was shut down, putting an end to its unethical operations.

During this process, Ajay took control of Digvijay's other

businesses. Due to the public sentiment and newfound trust in Ajay's leadership, these businesses thrived.

I also made sure to shed light on the unjust treatment of Mahesh, who had been falsely accused of being a paedophile when he had tried to help Ajay. Through our efforts, Mahesh's image was restored, and he finally received the justice he deserved.

MAHESH

I was sitting in the park with Ahana outside my house. The sun was still high in the sky, but its warmth was fading away as the evening settled in. Ahana and I were both wearing our favourite outfits—mine a light blue kurta, hers a bright yellow salwar kameez. Our conversation was light and casual, but in that moment there was a sense of peace in the air.

Just then, I heard my phone ringing from inside the house. I excused myself from our conversation and hurried inside. I picked up the phone to see that it was my beloved granddaughter, Jasmeen, calling me.

"Hi Dadu," she said.

I couldn't help but feel emotional hearing her voice after so long, and the tears began to flow.

"Hello beta," I said, controlling my tears, "How are you? My goodness, I've missed you so much! So very much!"

PARAG

I arrived at my destination, my hands gripping the steering wheel in anticipation. I had spent the last few weeks in a flurry of activity, not sure how to best handle the situation. It all seemed like a distant dream now.

Ajay had saved me, and for that, I was eternally grateful. Digvijay had wanted me to take all the blame for his wrongdoing, and if things had been made public, I would have been ruined. But Ajay had stepped in and helped me regain my reputation as a politician.

I also took advantage of my political image and saved Ahana from the murder charges of Digvijay. I hired the best lawyer in the country and helped him with all the facts to save Ahana from the charges of murder. It was all done in self-defence and that is what we proved in the court of law. It was difficult but thankfully a short fight.

I looked in the rear-view mirror, my reflection blurry in the dim light of day. I stepped out of the car and walked towards the main gate of the house. I paused before ringing the bell, my heart pounding in my chest.

The door opened before I could press the buzzer. Ahana stood there, her face lit up with a warm smile. We stood in silence for a moment, both of us hesitating. I was unsure of how to proceed, but I knew I had to do it. I had to talk to her.

She opened the door wider and gestured for me to come in. I stepped across the threshold, and as I did so, I felt a wave of relief wash over me. I was finally here, and I was finally ready to talk to her.

"I don't know whether you remember me or not, but we have met before," I said, to which Ahana smiled warmly.

"Of course, I remember you. Now come in, everyone is waiting for you," she replied, gently holding my hand and guiding me inside her house.